"Have you always lived here?"

Grant shrugged. "Maine is home. I always knew it was where I belonged."

"But didn't you ever aspire to more?" Morgan asked.

"I have my faith, my family and work I love. What more is there?"

Morgan didn't know how to respond to that. Grant seemed like a man who had found his place in the world and was content with it. There was no restlessness, no grasping, no struggle to meet some definition of worldly success. He was a man at peace with himself. She envied him that.

Morgan suddenly shivered, and she knew it was time to go. But she didn't want to. Here, in this man's presence, she felt a sense of calm, of caring, that was a balm to her soul. And she didn't want the moment to end.

Books by Irene Hannon

Love Inspired

*Home for the Holidays #6
*A Groom of Her Own #16
*A Family To Call Her Own #25
It Had To Be You #58
One Special Christmas #77
The Way Home #112
Never Say Goodbye #175
Crossroads #224
†*The Best Gift* #292
†*Gift from the Heart* #307
†*The Unexpected Gift* #319

*Vows
†Sisters & Brides

IRENE HANNON

is an award-winning author who has been a writer for as long as she can remember. She "officially" launched her career at the age of ten, when she was one of the winners in a "complete-the-story" contest conducted by a national children's magazine. More recently, Irene won the coveted RITA® Award for her 2002 Love Inspired book *Never Say Goodbye*. Irene, who spent many years in an executive corporate communications position with a Fortune 500 company, now devotes herself full-time to her writing career. In her "spare" time, she enjoys performing in community musical theater productions, singing in the church choir, gardening, cooking and spending time with family and friends. She and her husband, Tom—whom she describes as "my own romantic hero"—make their home in Missouri.

IRENE HANNON

THE UNEXPECTED GIFT

Steeple
Hill®

Published by Steeple Hill Books™

STEEPLE HILL BOOKS

Steeple
Hill®

ISBN 0-373-81233-7

THE UNEXPECTED GIFT

Copyright © 2005 by Irene Hannon

www.SteepleHill.com

Printed in U.S.A.

Though the mountains leave their place and the hills be shaken, My love shall never leave you.

—*Isaiah* 54:10

To the many special friends who have supported my writing career through the years—especially Caroline, Janice, Jo Ann and Lori—and to all of the readers who have taken the time to write me such wonderful, heartwarming letters. I read them all. Thank you!

Prologue

Morgan Williams frowned as she read the e-mail message on her Blackberry. Great. Just great. Her newest client at the agency was requesting a meeting first thing tomorrow to discuss ideas for the next ad campaign. Unfortunately, Morgan didn't have any. She'd been too busy with Aunt Jo's funeral to give the campaign more than a passing thought. Which wasn't good. And would not be looked upon kindly by her superiors. In her world, work came first. Period. To paraphrase the postal service motto, nothing—neither rain, nor snow, nor sleet…nor a funeral—should keep her from her appointed task. Not when she had her eye on a top spot in the firm.

Her frown deepened, and she typed in a reply, asking if the meeting could be delayed a day. Even then, she'd be scrambling for ideas.

But she'd come through. She always did. That's why she was on the fast track.

Morgan finished the e-mail and hit Send. As she leaned against the plush back of the settee in the attorney's elegant waiting room, she glanced impatiently at her watch. "I wish he'd hurry. I have a plane to catch."

A.J. turned from the window, which framed a row of flame-red maples against a brilliant St. Louis late-October sky. "Chill out, Morgan," she advised. "The advertising world can live without you for a few more hours."

Shooting her younger sister an annoyed look, Morgan rummaged in her purse for her cell phone. "Trust me, A.J. The business arena is nothing like your non-profit world. Hours do matter to us. So do minutes."

"More's the pity," A.J. responded in a mild tone, turning back to admire the view again. "Life is too short to be so stressed about things as fleeting as ad campaigns."

Morgan opened her mouth to respond, but Clare beat her to it. "Don't you think we should put our philosophical differences aside today, in respect for Aunt Jo?" she interjected in a gentle, non-judgmental tone.

Morgan and A.J. turned in unison toward their older sister, and A.J. grinned.

"Ever the peacemaker, Clare," she said, her voice tinged with affection.

"Somebody had to keep the two of you from doing each other bodily harm when we were growing up," Clare said with a smile. "And since I was the only one who didn't inherit mom's McCauley-red hair—and the temper that went with it—I suppose the job had to fall to me."

A.J. joined Morgan on the couch. "Okay. In honor of Aunt Jo, I declare a truce. How about it, Morgan?"

Hesitating only a second, Morgan ditched her cell phone in her purse. "Truce," she agreed with a grin. "Besides, much as I hate to admit that my kid sister is sometimes right, I am occasionally guilty of taking my job too seriously."

"Occasionally?" A.J. rolled her eyes.

"Enough, you two," Clare admonished with a smile.

"Okay, okay," A.J. said with a laugh. "I bet you whip those kids into shape whenever you substitute-teach. In a nice way, of course. Their regular teacher is probably astounded at their good behavior when she gets back."

Her smile fading, Clare looked down to fiddle with the strap on her purse. "I do my best.

But I still have a lot to learn. It's been so many years since I taught…it's harder some days than others."

A.J. and Morgan exchanged a look. "Hang in there, Clare," Morgan said. "We're here for you."

"It does get easier. Not overnight. But bit by bit. Trust me," A.J. added, her own voice a bit uneven.

As Clare reached over to squeeze A.J.'s hand, Morgan looked from one sister to the other. Both had known their share of trauma. More than their share, in fact. Yet they'd carried on, with courage and strength. She admired them for that, more than words could say. And she was also glad they were family. Because even though they had their differences, one thing remained steady. They always stood together, like the Three Musketeers—one for all and all for one. It gave Morgan a sense of comfort to know that her sisters loved her just as she was, and that she could count on them if she ever needed their support or help.

But she hadn't done much in recent years to earn their love, she acknowledged. She kept in touch, but her contact with them was sporadic at best. A call here or there, a card on special occasions. Which wasn't enough.

Family was important, after all. And with Mom and Dad gone they were all she had now. On occasions like this when they were all together, Morgan was reminded that she should make more of an effort to keep their bond strong. And each time, she left with good intentions of staying in closer contact. But the demands of her career always undermined her resolution.

The door to the inner office opened, interrupting her thoughts, and the sisters turned their heads in unison toward Seth Mitchell.

For a long moment the distinguished, gray-haired attorney standing in the doorway studied Jo Warren's three great-nieces with a look Morgan recognized at once. She'd seen it often enough in the business world. He was sizing them up. And Seth Mitchell was good at it. He didn't reveal a single emotion as he took in A.J.'s long, unruly strawberry-blond hair, eclectic attire and interested expression. When he looked at her, Morgan was sure he noticed the sleek, shoulder-length style of her copper-colored hair, her chic business attire and her impatient expression. As for Clare—no doubt she fared the best, Morgan concluded. Her honey-gold hair, which was swept back into an elegant chignon, complemented her designer suit and

Gucci purse. But did he also notice the deep, lingering sadness in her older sister's eyes?

She didn't have time to wonder, because he moved toward them. "Good morning, ladies. I'm Seth Mitchell. I recognize you from Jo's description—A.J., Morgan, Clare," he said, identifying the sisters in turn as he extended his hand to each. "Please accept my condolences on the loss of your aunt. She was a great lady."

They murmured polite responses, and he motioned toward his office. "If you're ready, we can proceed with the reading of the will."

He didn't speak again until they were all seated, at which point he picked up a hefty document. "I'll give each of you a copy of your great-aunt's will to take with you, so I don't think there's any reason to go through this whole document now. A lot of it is legalese, and there are some charitable bequests that you can review at your leisure. I thought we could restrict the formal reading to the section that affects each of you directly, if that's agreeable."

"Absolutely," Morgan replied. "My plane for Boston leaves in less than three hours. I know Clare needs to get back to Kansas City, and A.J. has a long drive to Chicago."

Seth looked at the other two sisters. When

they nodded their assent, he flipped through the document to a marked page and began to read.

"'Insofar as I have no living relatives other than my three great-nieces—the daughters of my sole nephew, Jonathan Williams, now deceased—I bequeath the bulk of my estate to them, in the following manner and with the following stipulations and conditions.

"'To Abigail Jeanette Williams, I bequeath half ownership of my bookstore in St. Louis, Turning Leaves, with the stipulation that she retain ownership for a minimum of six months and work full-time in the store during this period. The remaining half ownership I bequeath to the present manager, Blake Sullivan, with the same stipulation.

"To Morgan Williams, I bequeath half ownership of Serenity Point, my cottage in Seaside, Maine, providing that she retains her ownership for a six-month period following my death and that she spends a total of four weeks in residence at the cottage. During this time she is also to provide advertising and promotional assistance for Good Shepherd Camp and attend board meetings as an advisory member. The remaining half ownership of the cottage I bequeath to Grant Kincaid of Seaside, Maine.

"To Clare Randall, I bequeath my remaining

financial assets, except for those designated to be given to the charities specified in this document, with the stipulation that she serve as nanny for Nicole Wright, daughter of Dr. Adam Wright of Hope Creek, North Carolina, for a period of six months, at no charge to Dr. Wright.

"Should the stipulations and conditions for the aforementioned bequests not be fulfilled, the specified assets will be disposed of according to directions given to my attorney, Seth Mitchell. He will also designate the date on which the clock will begin ticking on the six-month period specified in my will.'" Seth lowered the document to his desk. "There you have it, ladies. I can provide more details on your bequests to each of you individually, but are there any general questions that I can answer?"

"Well, I might as well write mine off right now," Morgan said in disgust. "There's no way I can be away from the office for four days, let alone four weeks. And what is Good Shepherd Camp?"

"Who is this Dr. Wright?" Clare asked. "And what makes Aunt Jo think he would want me as a nanny?"

"When can I start?" A.J. asked.

"Let me take your questions and comments one at a time," Seth said. "Morgan, you have the

right to turn down the bequest, of course. But
I would advise you to get some legal and financial counsel first. Jo bought that property years
ago, when Seaside was just a quiet, backwater
village. The area is now a bustling tourist
mecca. So her property has increased signifi-
cantly in value. As for how to meet your aunt's
residence stipulation—I'm afraid I can't advise you on that. Good Shepherd is a summer
camp in Maine for children from troubled
homes. Your aunt has been involved with the organization for many years."

He went on to answer Clare's and A.J.'s questions, but Morgan tuned him out. This was so
like Aunt Jo, she fumed. In life, she hadn't ap-
proved of Morgan's single-minded pursuit of
success. In death, she'd done her best to derail
it. In all honesty, Morgan hadn't even expected
to be remembered in her great-aunt's will. Until
Seth Mitchell had called to tell her she was a
beneficiary, she'd expected nothing more than
a cursory remembrance of some sort, if that. Instead, it sounded as if she'd been left a wind-
fall. With strings. Strings that would require
her to juggle the demands of her career with
Aunt Jo's stipulations.

It was not a task she relished.

Seth paused, and she tuned him back in when

he began speaking again. "Let's officially start the clock for the six-month period on December 1. That will give you about a month to make plans. Now, are there any more general questions?"

The three women looked at him, looked at each other, then shook their heads

"Very well." He handed them each a manila envelope. "But do feel free to call if any come up as you review the will more thoroughly." He rose, signaling the end of the meeting, and extended his hand to each sister in turn. "Again, my condolences on the death of your great-aunt. Jo had a positive impact on countless lives and will be missed by many people. I know she loved each of you very much, and that she wanted you to succeed in claiming your bequests.

"Good luck, ladies."

As Morgan followed her sisters from the office, Seth Mitchell's final words echoed in her mind. Luck would help, of course.

But she knew it was going to take a whole lot more than that for her to find a way to claim her inheritance.

Chapter One

"You're working over Thanksgiving?"

Morgan heard the surprise—and disapproval—in Grant Kincaid's voice, and frowned in annoyance. It was the same reaction she'd gotten from A.J., who had made it clear that she thought her sister was a workaholic without a life. Morgan hadn't liked it then; she didn't like it now.

"I happen to be committed to my job," Morgan replied stiffly. "In my world, working on holidays is a way of life. That's how you get ahead."

She braced herself for another negative comment. But he surprised her.

"Well, just let me know when you plan to come up and I'll have the cottage ready," he said.

"I'll do that. In the meantime, I'd like to get an appraisal done on the property."

There was a note of caution in his voice when he responded. "May I ask why?"

Her patience waning, Morgan glanced at her watch. "It will be extremely difficult for me to meet the residency stipulation in my great-aunt's will, Mr. Kincaid. I have trouble taking off four days, let alone four weeks. So before I spend a lot of time and energy trying to figure out how to juggle my life to allow for several weeks in Maine, I want to make sure it's worth my while. Besides, we'll need to get an appraisal before we sell, anyway."

"You're planning to sell?" He made no attempt to disguise the shock in his voice.

"Of course. What would I do with a cottage in Maine?"

"Maybe the same thing your aunt did. Spend time here, relax, regain perspective. It's a beautiful spot."

Morgan gave a frustrated sigh. "I'm sure it's lovely, Mr. Kincaid. But as I explained, I have little time for that kind of thing."

"The cottage was very special to your aunt."

"I understand that. But holding on to a place I'll never use doesn't make good business sense. Of course you'd certainly be welcome to buy my share at the end of six months, assuming I even make it that far."

"That's kind of you. But the property is way out of my price range."

Was there a touch of sarcasm in his comment? Morgan couldn't be sure, but she didn't have time to waste wondering about it. She had a presentation to finalize for a meeting that would be starting in less than an hour. Further discussion of Aunt Jo's cottage would have to wait.

"Look, I need to run. We can talk about that at some point in the future. In the meantime, can you take care of the appraisal?"

"Yes."

"Fine. I'll try to get up to Maine soon. The cottage looks to be about a four-hour drive from Boston. Is that right?"

"More like five, if you're not familiar with the back roads."

"Okay. I'll try to make a weekend trip soon."

"I'll look forward to it."

This time there was no mistaking the sarcasm in his tone. Nor the fact that he didn't think much of her priorities. Just like her sister. Come to think of it, he and A.J. would have been ideal co-owners of the cottage, Morgan reflected. Too bad Aunt Jo hadn't paired them up.

Grant replaced the receiver and turned to find his father watching him.

"I take it that was Jo's great-niece?" Andrew Kincaid said.

"None other."

"Sounded like an interesting conversation from this end."

"Were you eavesdropping?" Grant asked with a smile.

"Of course. That's what family is for," he replied, his blue eyes twinkling.

Grant chuckled. He and his father didn't have many secrets. Nor did anyone in his extended family. He'd always been close to his sister, Kit, and her husband, Bill, the pastor at their church. And he doted on his fifteen-year-old twin nieces. He also had a deep love and affection for his uncle, who worked with him and his dad in the cabinet shop. They were a small but close-knit bunch.

Except for his mother, of course.

Which brought him back to Morgan Williams.

"Interesting is a good way to describe the conversation." He shook his head. "She's a piece of work."

"How so?"

"When I suggested she come up to take a look at the cottage over Thanksgiving, she told me she'd be working."

"On Thanksgiving?"

"My exact reaction. And she did *not* appreciate it."

"So when is she coming up?"

"Who knows? But in the meantime, she asked me to get an appraisal on the property, because she plans to sell."

The older man pondered that. "How do you feel about letting the place go?"

Grant shrugged, but his eyes were troubled. "There won't be much choice if she wants to sell, unless we can find someone who's willing to buy her half and take me on as co-owner."

"Maybe she'll change her mind when she sees it."

As Grant replayed their conversation in his mind, he shook his head. "I wouldn't place any bets on that. She's one tough cookie. A hardnosed businesswoman through and through. I can't figure out why Jo left the place to her."

His father pulled on a pair of work gloves. "I imagine she had her reasons. Jo was a smart lady. I can't remember her ever doing anything that didn't make sense."

"Well, there's always a first time." Grant reached for his own gloves. "Now let's go sort through that load of maple."

* * *

Morgan punched in the number for Good Shepherd Camp and drummed her fingers on the desk as she waited for someone to answer. At least this stipulation in her aunt's will should be manageable. Serving as an advisory member of a charitable board for six months and offering a bit of advice on a fund-raising drive was a piece of cake compared to spending four weeks in a remote cottage on the coast of Maine.

The phone continued to ring, and Morgan was just about to hang up when someone answered.

"Good Shepherd Camp," said a breathless female voice.

"Good morning. This is Morgan Williams. May I speak with the person in charge?"

Her crisp request was met with an amused chuckle. "You've got her. Mary Stanton. I'm the chief cook and bottle washer around here in the off-season. How can I help you?"

"Actually, it's more like how I can help you." Morgan explained the provision in Aunt Jo's will. "So I just need to see how you'd like me to get involved," she finished.

"I'd heard about your great-aunt's death," the woman said, her voice sympathetic. "She was a long-time supporter of the camp. Going back well before my time, in fact. I'm sorry for your loss. And ours."

"I'm sure my great-aunt will be missed by many people." Morgan kept her reply innocuous.

"I'm a bit surprised by the stipulation in her will, but we're always happy to have more help. We run this operation on a shoestring. There are just a couple of full-time employees—me, in the office, and Joe Carroll at the camp, who does maintenance. He and his wife, Elizabeth, live there year-round. We beef up the paid staff a bit in the summer, but most of our counselors are volunteers. So we're always looking for free help." She paused as if considering the best next step. "I'll tell you what. Let me have the president of the board give you a call to discuss your involvement. That's really who you should talk to, since the board makes all the decisions, anyway. I'm just a worker bee," the woman said with a laugh.

"That would be great. Let me give you my number." As she did so, Clark, her boss, appeared at her door and began making urgent motions. "Um, look, I need to go. It seems some sort of crisis has arisen here."

"Of course. We'll be in touch. And thank you again. Good Shepherd Camp is a very worthwhile effort. Your time won't be wasted."

Morgan wasn't sure she agreed. No matter how much or how little time she spent on Aunt Jo's pet project, it was still time away from her job. And since she had her sights set on a top spot in the firm in the not-too-distant future, she couldn't afford to let her focus waver.

But unfortunately, Aunt Jo had done her best to see that it did.

As Grant stared at the message from Mary Stanton, then read it again, a slow smile spread over his face. Morgan Williams must just love this, he thought with perverse enjoyment. Not only had Jo put a residency requirement in her bequest, she'd ordered her niece to help out at Good Shepherd. Morgan Williams didn't strike him as the type of woman who liked to take orders. Which Jo must have known. So what was the older woman up to?

Grant didn't have a clue. But it didn't matter. Extra hands were always welcome at Good Shepherd, willing or not. As president of the board, he'd done his share of recruiting volunteers, and it wasn't easy. People these days, even those who called themselves Christians, were too busy to take time out to help others. So he was glad Jo had recruited this "volunteer" for him. Morgan Williams might be reluctant, but they were in dire need of her expertise. The camp's financial situation was precarious at best, and Grant was willing to do just about anything to shore up the coffers. Even conspiring with Jo's workaholic niece.

The bell over the front door of the cabinet shop jangled, and Grant looked up to find his uncle juggling a large white bag, a tray of drinks and a stack of mail.

"I ran into Chuck at the sandwich shop and offered to take our mail off his hands," Uncle Pete said, his usual ruddy face even redder, thanks to the biting wind. "December's a bear for the postal service. Figured I'd save him three stops. Where's Andrew?"

"In the back."

The older man peered at the slip of paper in Grant's hand. "I see you got your message."

"You could have let it roll to the answering machine."

"Never did trust those things. Come on back. Let's eat."

Eying the bag, Grant shook his head, exasperation mingling with affection. "You don't have to bring me lunch, Uncle Pete. I can take care of myself."

"So what're you going to eat today?"

"I'll grab something on the way to Brunswick."

The older man gave a skeptical snort. "I've heard that before. What'd you eat yesterday?"

Grant felt his neck grow warm. "I skipped lunch yesterday."

"That's what I figured. Come on back and eat. No more arguments."

"How about a thank-you instead?"

"Not necessary," Uncle Pete said, his voice gruff. "Wish I could do more, in fact. You've had a tough time, still do, and if I want to help you out in little ways, let me. Come on back."

Before Grant could respond, Uncle Pete headed for the back room. Grant took his time following. *Thank you, Lord, for this loving family,* he prayed, as he had so many times in the past two-and-a-half years. *I couldn't make it without them.*

By the time Grant got to the worn pine table where the three men had shared so many lunches, his father had cleared off a spot and Uncle Pete was spreading out the food and sorting through the mail. He looked at the two men with affection as he moved a T-square and hand-drawn plans for a mahogany entertainment center off to the side. His bachelor uncle and his father had lived together ever since Grant had gone off to college. It had been a good arrangement, providing both men with much-needed companionship. They'd invited Grant to join them a couple of years ago, but for now he wanted to remain in the tiny bungalow where he'd known so much joy. Leaving it would somehow seem to signal a loss of hope.

Yet there were times when he was tempted to accept their offer. As much as he liked quiet, and as comfortable as he was with solitude, the loneliness…no, *emptiness* was a better word, he decided…sometimes got to him. Maybe someday he would move in with them, if… Grant cut off that thought. He wouldn't let himself go there. He never did.

"Looks like your mother remembered your birthday," Uncle Pete remarked, handing Grant a blue envelope with the logo of a well-known greeting card company on the back.

Grant took it without comment, laid it aside, and turned his attention to his turkey sandwich.

"It's nice that she remembered," his father commented.

"Yeah. Only a week late." There was a bitter edge to Grant's voice.

His father reached over and laid a work-worn hand on Grant's shoulder. "Let it go, son. It's ancient history now."

"I can't forget what she did, Dad. I don't know how you can."

"I haven't forgotten. But I made my peace with it a long time ago. It's time you did, too."

Uncle Pete generally watched this exchange without a word. It had been replayed numerous times over the years—and always with the same result. But this time he spoke. "Andrew's right, Grant. Give it to the Lord. Get on with your life."

"What she did was wrong, Uncle Pete."

"I'm not sayin' it was right or wrong. Just that it's over. Holdin' on to anger don't help nobody."

Grant crumpled the paper that had held his sandwich, then tossed it into the bag. "I wish I could. You two put me to shame."

"Hardly. What you've done these past two-and-a-half years would have finished me off," his father said.

"I doubt that. I come from strong stock. Besides, people do what they have to do."

"Not everybody," Uncle Pete disagreed. "And you've never wavered all this time, either. You're just as faithful now as you were at the beginning."

Uncomfortable with the praise, Grant glanced at his watch. "Which reminds me. I need to run. I'll be back by about two-thirty."

"Take your time, son. And give her our best."

"I always do. See you guys later. Thanks for lunch, Uncle Pete."

"Glad to do it. Don't forget to return that call."

That brought a smile to Grant's face. "It's right at the top of my list as soon as I get back."

As he walked down the quiet hallway, Grant raised his hand in greeting to the woman behind the desk. "Hi, Ruth. Any change?" He'd been asking the same question for more than two years. And getting the same answer.

"No. She's holding her own."

He continued down the hall, stopping outside the familiar room where he'd spent so many hours. He took a deep breath, then stepped inside, closing the door halfway behind him.

After all this time, he still harbored a faint hope that one day he'd walk into the extended-care facility and find his wife waiting to greet him with her sweet smile. But he was always disappointed. Though less so now. Hope, once strong, had dimmed as days became weeks, and months became years.

Grant moved beside the bed and stared down at the face of the woman who had stolen his heart, the woman to whom he had pledged his life six-and-a-half years ago—for better or

worse—before God. And he'd meant every
word of that vow. He just hadn't expected the
worst to happen so quickly, just four short years
into their marriage. Now the woman around
whom he'd planned his future, the woman with
whom he'd hoped to raise a family, the woman
with whom he'd wanted to grow old, lay sus-
pended between life and death, her once-strong
limbs wasted, her passionate, laughter-filled
eyes shuttered.

Closing his eyes, Grant took a steadying
breath. *Lord, give me strength to carry on,* he
prayed. *I don't know why you've given Christine and me this cross to bear, but I place my
trust in you. Please continue to watch over us.*

He left his eyes closed for a long moment,
drawing what solace he could from the prayer
he uttered every day at his wife's bedside. Then
he leaned down to kiss her cool forehead,
reaching over to take her unresponsive hand in
his. "Hi, Christine. It's Grant. I brought a new
novel I thought you'd enjoy. And the Bible, of
course. But first I'll give you all the family
news."

He sat beside her, keeping her hand in his,
and talked with her about his surprising bequest from Jo, filled her in on the latest com-
missions they'd received at the shop, and

reminded her how much everyone missed her. It was a routine he'd begun soon after the accident, at the suggestion of her doctors, who had told him that comatose people could sometimes hear voices. They'd encouraged him to share his day with her, to read to her, saying that it might make a difference in her recovery. They didn't push him to do that anymore. But he still continued the practice.

At the end of an hour, he opened the Bible to Psalms and picked up where he'd left off the day before. He always ended his visits with the Good Book, and today the verse seemed especially appropriate.

"'Only in God be at rest, my soul, for from Him comes my hope,'" Grant read, his voice mellow and deep and steady. "'He only is my rock and my salvation, my stronghold; I shall not be disturbed. With God is my safety and my glory, he is the rock of my strength; my refuge is in God. Trust in Him at all times, O my people! Pour out your hearts before Him; God is our refuge.'"

As Grant closed the book, he let the words soothe his soul. Then he stood and once more leaned down to press his lips to Christine's forehead.

"Rest well, sweetheart. Never forget how much I love you," he whispered.

Grant moved to the door, taking one final look at Christine's still form. As he stepped outside, Ruth was just passing by.

"See you tomorrow," she said.

Grant nodded. "I'll be here."

Chapter Two

"Morgan Williams."

As her voice came over the wire, Grant's lip tipped up into wry grin. He'd tried her office number first, somehow knowing she'd still be there at eight o'clock at night. And her tone captured her personality to perfection. Crisp. Pleasant. Efficient. Businesslike. Except the pleasant part might go out the window when she found out why he was calling.

"Ms. Williams, it's Grant Kincaid."

He could almost hear her frown over the phone, and when she spoke her voice held an edge of impatience. "What can I do for you?"

"I think the question is, what can *you* do for *me?*"

Her sigh was audible. "Look, Mr. Kincaid, I

don't have time for riddles. Is there a problem with the cottage?"

"First of all, since I expect we'll be talking quite a bit for the next few months, can we dispense with the formality? Just call me Grant. Second, this isn't about the cottage. It's about Jo's requirement that you assist with Good Shepherd Camp."

"How do you know about that?" She sounded surprised—and wary.

"I'm president of the board."

He expected her to groan. But if she did, she hid it well.

"I see," she replied tersely.

"I understand from Mary that you are to provide advertising and promotional assistance for Good Shepherd and attend board meetings as an advisory member for the next six months. Is that correct?"

"Yes."

"Do you know anything about the camp?"

"No."

Nor did she want to, if her tone was any indication. "I'll tell you what. Why don't I send you some literature? That will give you a lot of background. The board doesn't meet in December, so you're off the hook until January. But you'll be a welcome addition. The camp is in pretty serious financial straits, and we need to come up with a way to generate significant income. Some sort of advertising or promotional campaign may be the answer. So we can use your expertise."

"I don't have any experience in the non-profit area, Mr. Kincaid. So don't get your hopes up."

"It's Grant," he reminded her. "And any help you can provide will be much appreciated. The camp is a very worthwhile cause, and we want to do everything possible to make sure it stays solvent. A lot of lives have been changed for the better because of Good Shepherd. All of the kids who go there have some kind of problem. They come from broken or abusive homes, or they've had run-ins with the law, or they have minor physical disabilities that have led to social or emotional problems. The camp experience has been a godsend for countless young people."

Even though Morgan had little personal interest in the project, she was struck by the passion and conviction in Grant's voice. She may not like the man, but she admired his willingness to help those less fortunate.

"I'll look over whatever you want to send when I have a minute," she promised.

"Okay. On a different subject, any idea when you'll be coming up to the cottage?"

Good question. She'd gotten the appraisal, and Seth Mitchell had been right. The property was far too valuable to toss aside. So she had to give this her best shot. She glanced at her schedule, which was packed, as always. But Christmas was on a Saturday, she noted. Which meant the office would be closed Friday and Monday. So she could make a long weekend of it without missing any official work time.

"Probably over the holiday. Would you be available to meet on Christmas Eve?"

"Sorry, no. I have family activities planned for that day," he said, making no attempt to hide his disapproval. "Could we make it Monday?"

"How about Sunday?" she countered.

"I usually reserve Sunday for God. And family."

Morgan expelled a frustrated breath. She'd hoped to leave on Sunday and put in a full day at the office on Monday, even though the firm was closed. But Grant didn't sound as if he was going to bend. "Okay," she relented. "As long as we can make it early." At least she'd be able to get in half a day of work.

"No problem. If you give me your number, I'll fax you directions to the cottage."

After complying, Morgan ended the call and tried to turn her attention back to the latest campaign she was developing for a new brand of soft drink. But it wasn't easy.

Although, she'd more or less resigned herself to the fact that she'd have to be civil to Grant for the next few months, however much his obvious disapproval rankled her, she'd consoled herself with the knowledge that she really wouldn't have to communicate much with him. However, if he was chairman of the board of Good Shepherd, there was very little chance she could avoid talking with him on a regular basis. Which was *not* a good thing, since they were about as compatible as the proverbial oil and water.

Plus, the clock had started ticking on Aunt Jo's six-month window, and Morgan figured she'd be spending two, maybe three days at the cottage in December. Tops. It didn't take a math genius to figure out that at this rate, there was no way she was going to meet the four-week residency requirement.

She had to come up with a better plan.

So much for a good night's sleep. As the crash of the surf and the howling wind outside Aunt Jo's cottage jarred her awake for the umpteenth time, Morgan peered bleary-eyed at the illuminated face of her travel alarm. Twelve-thirty.

Merry Christmas, she thought grumpily.

She scrunched her pillow under her head, pulled the blankets up to her ears, and tried by sheer force of will to ignore the unfamiliar sounds of the elements raging outside her window. But it was no use. It was too noisy and she was too tense.

Morgan had ended up working until midafternoon on Christmas Eve, and by the time she'd arrived in Maine and wandered for what seemed like hours on the back roads in search of Aunt Jo's isolated cottage, she'd been forced to contend not only with the dark, but with sleet, snow and ferocious wind.

When she'd at last pulled to a stop in front of the weathered clapboard structure, she'd had to sit in her car for a full minute until her nerves stopped vibrating. She'd ruined her twenty-dollar manicure as she'd tried without success to pry open her frozen trunk. She'd slipped and slid toward the door in her high-fashion, expensive boots, which had not been designed for the backwoods of Maine. And she'd lost her Saks scarf in a tug-of-war with the gale-force winds.

It had not been an auspicious arrival.

Taking a deep breath, Morgan tried to force herself to relax, but sleep remained elusive. Finally, when the first light of dawn began to creep in under the window shades, she gave up. If she was the praying type, she'd send a desperate plea heavenward for a fortifying cup of coffee. As it was she just crossed her fingers and headed for the kitchen.

But a quick search of the pantry turned up only Spartan supplies—two cans of soup, some stale crackers, salt and pepper, a can of tuna and a couple of stray tea bags. She wasn't much of a tea drinker, but at this point she'd settle for anything with caffeine.

As she filled a mug with water and put it in the microwave, she glanced around. The cottage might have appeared rustic on the outside, but Aunt Jo had created an impressive kitchen. Though compact, it was very functional, with state-of-the-art stainless-steel appliances. And the adjacent eating area, tucked into a bay window that afforded a clear view of the churning waves in the gun-metal-gray water of early dawn, was inviting.

After making her tea, Morgan wandered into the living room. Despite their philosophical differences, she had to admit that Aunt Jo had good taste. The bright walls were hung with what looked like original paintings and watercolors, and plaid and chintz fabrics in cheerful colors covered the upholstered furniture. A small deck opened off the living room, again affording a panoramic vista of the ocean just seventy or eighty feet away.

As she stood at the window sipping her tea, dawn began to stain the sky an ethereal pink. She watched, transfixed, as the color deepened and spread, dispersing as the sun crept over the horizon. It seemed the storm had passed, for the sky was clear now and the wind had all but disappeared. As the sun rose higher, its rays reached out to touch the ice-encased trees and the snow-laden boughs of the fir trees, turning the scene into a magical, sparkling wonderland and filling the world with dazzling, brilliant light.

Which was a good thing. Because all at once the lights in the cottage flickered and went out.

With a look of dismay—and a sudden feeling of foreboding—Morgan walked over to the phone and picked it up. Dead. Why wasn't she surprised? So far, nothing about this trip had gone as planned. And with the electricity out, she could pretty much write off the possibility of getting much work done once her laptop battery gave out, she thought in disgust.

Setting her tea aside, she fumbled in her purse for her cell phone. She didn't have much hope that it would function in this remote area, but it was worth a try. She'd promised to call Clare and A.J., who were spending Christmas together in North Carolina.

Much to her surprise, she got a signal, and a moment later Clare answered.

"Morgan! Did you get to Aunt Jo's cottage okay? We heard on the news that there was a pretty bad storm in Maine, and we've been worried."

"I'm here, safe and sound," Morgan assured her.

"So how's the cottage?"

"Remote. Isolated. And without electricity or phone right now. I'm on my cell."

"Do you have heat?"

"I spotted a kerosene heater, so I should be okay. This must happen on a regular basis."

"So what are you going to do today?"

Morgan dropped into a chintz-covered chair. "Well, I'd planned to work, but without electricity my laptop won't last long."

"Maybe you could think about going to church. After all, it *is* Christmas. Remember how we all used to go together early in the morning, then come home and open presents? And Mom always made a wonderful dinner. I can still taste her roast lamb and oven-browned potatoes."

Morgan glanced at the cans of soup and tuna she'd taken out of the pantry, along with the stale crackers. It was a far cry from the holiday meals of her childhood, when she'd been surrounded by family in a house filled with love.

"Yeah, I remember," she replied, her lips curving into a wistful smile. "Those were good years."

"I wish you were here, Morgan. We miss you. And I hate for you to spend Christmas alone."

"I miss you guys, too. But I'm used to being alone, so don't worry about me. Can you put A.J. on?"

"Sure."

After a few seconds of silence, her younger sister spoke. "So what's this about working on Christmas?"

"Don't start with me, A.J.," Morgan warned.

"Hey, I only have your best interests at heart. Nobody should work on Christmas. It's a day for God and family. So just chill out and relax for once. Maybe even go to church, like Clare suggested. It couldn't hurt, you know."

"I haven't decided yet what I'm going to do."

"What are you having for dinner?"

Again, Morgan glanced at her meager supplies. She'd planned to stop and pick up a few things during the drive yesterday, but she'd gotten a late start, and when the weather turned bad she'd just kept going. She'd tossed a couple of frozen microwave dinners in the car with her luggage, but even if she could get the trunk open, the dinners weren't going to be of much use without electricity.

"I'm not sure yet."

"We're having roast chicken with garlic mashed potatoes, and Clare made a wonderful chocolate mousse for dessert."

Morgan's mouth started to water. "Think of me while you're eating."

"You know we will. Listen, Morgan, Clare was right. We miss you."

"I miss you, too. How's it going at the book-shop?"

"Okay, I guess." A.J. said with a chuckle. "But I think I'm driving my partner, Mr. Conventional, nuts. He's the Oxford-shirt-wearing, let's-plan-everything-out-down-to-the-last-de-tail type."

Morgan laughed. "And how's Clare doing with her assignment from Aunt Jo?"

"She seems to be ensconced in the Wright household. But I'd say she has her work cut out for her with the good doctor and his problem child."

"Well, tell her I wish her luck. And stay in touch, okay?"

"You, too. Merry Christmas."

As the line went dead, Morgan felt oddly bereft. She'd told Clare that she was used to being alone, and that was true enough. She liked her independence, and she'd created the precise life she wanted. But as she recalled the happy Christmases of her youth, she wished now that she could have found a way to join her sisters for the holiday. All at once the notion of spending the entire day alone, with only her work for company, held no appeal. Maybe she'd drive into Seaside and try to scrounge up some food. And if she saw a church, maybe—just maybe— she'd stop. After all, as both A.J. and Clare had reminded her, it *was* Christmas.

The trunk of her car was more cooperative this morning, and after a quick shower and change of clothes, Morgan tackled the drive into Seaside. The snowcovered roads were far easier to negotiate in the daylight, and within fifteen minutes she was in the tiny town. Maybe she'd find a nice restaurant or café and have a decent Christmas dinner after all, she thought, her sprits rising as she turned onto the main street.

But there was one little problem.

The streets were deserted and everything was closed and locked up.

As Morgan sat in her car debating her next

move, a tall white spire in the distance caught her eye. She wasn't in the mood for church, but a twinge of guilt about her lapsed faith niggled at her conscience. And it wasn't as if she had anything else to do. Including eat, she thought, with one more glum look around the shuttered town. Besides, it might be nice to attend services, for old time's sake. If nothing else, it would break up what otherwise promised to be a long, empty day. At least she could check it out. If she happened upon a service, great. If not…well, then it wasn't meant to be.

But as Morgan drove past the church, the steady influx of people made it clear that she was just in time for a ten o'clock service. A wry smile tipped up the corners of her mouth. Clare and A.J. would be pleased to find their wayward sister back in the fold—at least for one day.

Morgan found a parking spot down the street and made her way toward the tall spire that rose in splendor toward the cobalt-blue sky. As she slipped into the back of the spruce- and poinsettia-bedecked church, trying to be as inconspicuous as possible, the choir was singing a pre-service program of familiar carols. And with sudden vividness and poignancy, memories of her childhood came rushing back—

memories of the warm and loving family she had been blessed with, of a life that was simple but good, of the sense of security she'd always felt as she'd observed the steady, deep love between her parents.

Over the years, those happy, younger days had become just a distant recollection, but today the memories were startling in their intensity, perhaps because the setting reminded her of the Christmas services they'd all attended together in a church very similar to this one. It had been a holiday ritual.

But everything had changed forever the year her father died. Her sense of security had been shattered as her mother struggled to hang on to the farm her husband had loved. Clare had gone off to college. And life had never been the same again. She had left, when the time came, without a backward glance. Yet in this place, on this day, she wished she could recapture that sense of closeness, of family, that had once been such an integral part of her life. Her eyes grew misty, and she bowed her head, hoping no one would observe her uncharacteristic display of emotion.

But she wasn't quick enough. Grant was making his way back down the aisle to retrieve his father's glasses from the car when he noticed the striking woman with the dark copper-colored hair seated in a back corner, alone. In the instant before she bowed her head, he caught the glimmer of unshed tears in her eyes. His step faltered, but he quickly regained his stride. The woman was a stranger to him, and whatever her problem, it was none of his concern.

Still, he was curious. He knew most of the members of the congregation, even the ones who only attended services on special days. In fact, he knew most, if not all, of the year-round residents in town. And though Seaside was becoming a summertime mecca for those seeking peace and quiet, it had few visitors in the off season. The woman could be someone's relative, visiting for the holiday, he supposed. But if that was the case, why was she here alone? Especially on a day that most people spent with those they loved?

Grant knew he should just forget about the woman. He'd probably never see her again. But his brief glimpse of her had left him disturbed. Because in her eyes he'd seen what *he* had often experienced these past two-and-a-half years, despite his faith and the love and support of his extended family. Loss. Abandonment. Emptiness. And the sense that things would never be the same again.

Grant knew there was nothing he could do about his own situation except pray. Which he did. Every day. And that gave him great comfort.

But from the desolate look in her eyes, he somehow sensed that the solitary woman in the back of church didn't have that kind of faith to rely on, that despite her presence here today, she didn't expect to find any solace in the Lord. And perhaps she wouldn't even try.

So he did it for her.

Lord, please watch over Your daughter, who seems in need of comfort. Let her feel Your healing presence and give her guidance, as You have done for me. And on this Christmas Day, don't let her feel alone or abandoned. Instead, let her feel Your love and care in a tangible way. Amen.

Chapter Three

The low-battery light gave an ominous blink, and as Morgan shut down her laptop in frustration, her stomach rumbled. Again.

Her foray into Seaside to buy food had been useless, so she'd had to make do with the meager provisions in the cottage. And she was rationing those. Which wasn't easy, since her last real meal had been a late lunch yesterday. So far, she'd eaten one can of cold soup and a few crackers, all the while thinking about the meal A.J. and Morgan had planned. The pitiful can of soup, tin of tuna and handful of crackers that remained just depressed her, so she knew she needed to do something to distract herself. Namely, more work.

Her face resolute, she moved her laptop aside, reached for her bulging briefcase, and withdrew the latest layouts and copy for an up-coming ad campaign. Looking at photos of toothpaste and reading about the merits of the product wasn't the most exciting activity for Christmas Day, but it had to be done sooner or later. And since she had nothing else planned for the day, she might as well get it over with.

But as Morgan tried to focus on the layouts, she found her attention wandering to the scene outside the bay window. It was just as lovely in the early afternoon as it had been this morning. The view of the sea was framed by a few fir trees, and there appeared to be a small beach. The rough water was dotted with frothy whitecaps that peaked and dissolved in rapid succession, and the vast expanse of open sea was mesmerizing. She set her pen aside and propped her chin in her hand, the ad copy forgotten for the moment.

A sudden knock on the door startled her out of her reverie, and she looked toward it in sur-prise—and with more than a little trepidation. No one in town knew she was here except Grant Kincaid. And he was unlikely to make an ap-pearance on a holiday, she thought wryly. In Boston, she never answered the door without having the security guard in her building screen visitors. However, she didn't have that luxury out here. And this was a pretty isolated spot.

She reached for her cell phone, then made her way to the door and checked for a peephole. No luck. She moved to the window. A pickup truck was parked next to her sporty car, but she couldn't get a glimpse of her visitor from this angle.

Another knock sounded, this time with a bit more force, and she moved back to the door. At least there was a chain lock. Not that that would do her much good if someone was determined to get in. But it would slow them down while she called 911.

Sliding back the chain, Morgan opened the door just enough to peer out with one eye. A man with vivid blue eyes and neatly trimmed sandy brown hair stood on the other side, dressed in a wool topcoat with a scarf wrapped around his neck. He appeared to be several inches taller than Morgan, maybe close to six feet. And he definitely did not look like a derelict.

"May I help you?" she said, her voice muffled through the door.

"I'm Grant Kincaid. May I come in?"

Morgan's eyes widened. "Of course. Sorry for the caution, but I'm a big-city girl. I wasn't expecting anyone today." She slid the lock back, then moved behind the door as she opened it to give him access to the small entry area.

Stepping inside, Grant pulled off his gloves while she shut the door behind him. "Sorry to disturb you on Christmas, but…" His voice died as he turned and found himself face to face with the woman he'd seen in church. The one who had been fighting off tears, who had looked so alone and sad. Which was not at all the image he'd formed of Morgan Williams. In his mind, he'd come to think of her as cold, calculating and rather hard. This slender woman, dressed in black slacks and a soft angora sweater the exact color of her jade-green eyes, didn't look hard at all.

But there was surprise on both sides The man with whom she shared ownership of this cottage wasn't at all what Morgan had expected, either. For some reason she'd thought he would be older. But he looked to be only in his late thirties. And what was the reason for that odd expression on his face? As the silence lengthened, she grew uncomfortable. "Is something wrong?" she asked at last.

Grant forced himself to take a deep breath. "Sorry for staring. I was expecting a stranger, but I saw you in church this morning."

"A rare occurrence, I assure you," Morgan

told him, feeling hot color steal up her neck. "But it *is* Christmas. And I didn't have anything else to do. With the electricity out, I knew I wouldn't get much work done today once my laptop battery died. I see you found my scarf."

He held it out. "A fir tree out front was wearing it. The wind here can be pretty fierce."

"So I discovered last night. Thanks for rescuing this." She draped the black cashmere scarf over a convenient chair. "What brings you over on a holiday?" she asked, emphasizing the last word.

She was sounding more and more like the Morgan he'd dealt with before, Grant thought.

"I tried to call several times yesterday to make sure you'd arrived safely and had settled in, but you never answered. Then, when I called this morning, I discovered the phones weren't working. I also heard the electricity was out in parts of the peninsula, and Jo's cottage is often affected when that happens. So I just wanted to make sure you were okay." He glanced toward the fireplace. "I laid a fire in the grate, but I see you discovered the back-up kerosene heaters. Is everything else okay?"

Morgan looked at the fireplace. She hadn't even noticed the stacked kindling, waiting to be lit. She was touched by the thoughtful gesture—and by his visit. Even though it was Christmas, Grant had gone out of his way to check on her. For the first time since his arrival, there was genuine warmth in her voice when she replied.

"Yes, thank you. I'm sorry to have interrupted your holiday."

"I was on my way to my sister's, so it wasn't a problem. Did you find the candles?" He started to pull his gloves back on.

"I didn't even look. It was already light when the electricity went out."

"There should be some on the bottom shelf of the credenza by the table. Let me check."

As he moved through the living room and into the dining area, he glanced at the table. Morgan was sure his perceptive eyes missed nothing—neither the ad copy spread across the surface nor the soup, tuna and crackers. She expected him to make some comment about working on Christmas, but when he turned back to her, his question surprised her. "Is that your dinner?"

"I planned to stop on the way up and get a few things, but I left the office late and the weather turned bad, so I just kept driving. I have a couple of frozen microwave dinners, though, if the electricity ever comes back on."

"That could take a while."

"Well, at least I won't have to worry about gaining weight over the holiday," she said with a rueful smile. "Besides, I'm sure the stores in town will be open tomorrow. I can stock up on what I need then."

But that didn't solve her problem today. Instead of responding, Grant turned and pulled open the door of the credenza, crouching down to check out the bottom shelf—and buy himself some time. He and Morgan might be reluctant partners with major philosophical differences, but he didn't feel right about leaving her alone to eat tuna and a bowl of cold soup on Christmas Day. Not when Kit always made enough food for an army and would be the first to invite Morgan to join them if she was here. Even though Morgan wouldn't be among Grant's first choice of holiday guests, he couldn't in good conscience leave her out in the cold, figuratively speaking. Not after just listening this morning to the familiar Christmas tale about no room in the inn. And not after his prayer in church, when he'd asked the Lord to let Morgan feel His love and care in a tangible way. It seems that he'd been appointed the instrument to make that happen. Maybe God had a sense of humor, he thought, a smile quirking the corners of his mouth.

Standing, he brushed off his hands. "Looks like you're well-fixed for candles. And I found a flashlight, too." He flicked it on and off, verifying that the battery was still working, then set it on the top of the credenza.

"Thanks again for stopping by," Morgan said.

"Look, why don't you join us for dinner?" Grant said before his charitable impulse deserted him. "My sister, Kit, always makes plenty, and she won't mind one more guest."

Startled, Morgan shook her head. "I couldn't do that. It would be too much of an imposition, especially on Christmas. Besides, I'm not that hungry. This will be fine. But I do appreciate the thought."

Okay. He'd done his Christian duty by inviting her to dinner, and she'd refused. So he was off the hook. He could walk away and enjoy the afternoon with his family, Grant rationalized.

But for some reason, the image of Morgan in church, her eyes glistening with unshed tears, kept replaying in his mind. She didn't strike him as someone who often gave in to such displays of emotion. Although she seemed to be fine now, he couldn't forget that moment in church. Or the pain he'd seen in her eyes. And for that reason, even more than basic Christian charity, he felt the need to make one more try.

"Are you sure I can't tempt you with prime rib and glazed carrots and homemade rolls, not to mention a fabulous white chocolate raspberry cheesecake?"

Morgan's resolution wavered. She glanced at the proofs spread across the table, then at her meager dinner. Neither were appealing. But she couldn't just barge in on Grant's family. It wouldn't be right. "I can't do that to your sister, Grant. But I do appreciate the invitation."

Hesitating only for a moment, he reached into his pocket and withdrew a cell phone.

"What are you doing?" she asked, puzzled.

"Calling Kit. I'll double check, if that will make you feel better about it."

"Oh, no, please don't put her on the spot like…"

"Kit? It's Grant. Listen, I'm at the cottage with Jo's niece. There's no electricity here and she didn't have a chance to stop and buy any groceries. All she's got is a can of soup and some tuna." There was a pause before Grant spoke again. "That's what I told her. But she doesn't want to impose." Another pause. "Okay. I'll put her on."

He held the phone out to Morgan, who had no choice but to take it.

"This is Morgan."

"Morgan? Kit Adams. I hear you're in need of a meal." The woman's voice was friendly and open.

"As a matter of fact, I'm not. I told Grant that what I had was fine. I'm sorry he bothered you."

"He'd be a lot sorrier if he hadn't and I found out later what you had for Christmas dinner. Trust me, I have enough food to feed a dozen people, let alone eight. Please come. Jo was very special to us, and she always came for dinner if she was here on a holiday. We'd be honored to have you in her place."

Grant was leaning against the island that separated the kitchen from the dining area, arms folded across his chest, an I-told-you-so look on his face when she looked his way.

There didn't seem to be any polite way to decline the invitation. Not that Morgan wanted to. As the day had worn on, her thoughts had drifted with increasing frequency to A.J. and Clare and Christmases past. She'd felt more and more alone, and her work had grown less and less appealing. Now, thanks to Grant and his sister, she had another option.

"All right. If you're sure it's no trouble?"

"None at all. We'll see you in a few minutes."

Hitting the Off button, Morgan handed the

phone back to Grant. "Your sister is very persuasive."

For the first time since he'd arrived he gave her a genuine smile, and Morgan felt her heart beat double-time. Of course she'd noticed that Grant was a nice-looking man. But that smile…it transformed his face, and in the blink of an eye he went from nice-looking to heart-stopping handsome. Morgan met lots of attractive men in her business, but most of them *knew* they were good-looking. The appealing thing about Grant Kincaid was that he seemed completely unaware of his charm. Which made it all the more potent.

"Tell me about it. Kit is very diplomatic but single-minded. Most of the time she accomplishes whatever she sets out to do," Grant replied, his voice tinged with affection. "How soon can you be ready to leave? Kit is pretty laid-back about most things, but when she plans a big dinner, she expects her guests to be on time." He checked his watch, revealing a crisp white cuff and gold cuff link below the sleeve of a dark-gray suit. "I figure we've got thirty minutes, at best."

Morgan looked from his formal attire to her black pants and angora sweater, feeling underdressed. "I didn't bring any fancy clothes for this weekend."

He gave her a quick but thorough once-over. "You're fine just like that. I'm going to change into more casual clothes when I get to Kit's. I just went right from church to…I had another stop to make."

"In that case, give me five minutes."

Morgan took only enough time to run a comb through her hair and touch up her makeup before rejoining Grant in the living room. He stood when she entered, then reached for her coat and held it as she slid her arms inside.

"Thanks," she murmured, turning to face him as she buttoned it. "I'll just follow you there."

"It might be better if I drove you. These back roads can be tricky."

She smiled, but she wanted to be able to leave at the time of her choosing without disrupting the party for anyone else. When she spoke, her voice was firm. "I found that out last night, after I drove in circles for an hour. But I've already been to town today and I have a better sense of direction now. Thank you for offering, though."

Given the determined tilt of her chin and the uncompromising expression in her eyes, it was clear that her mind was made up. So Grant didn't push. "Okay. Let's head out."

He took her arm as they made their way across the slippery drive, his grip tightening when she lost her footing on a patch of ice.

When he glanced at her boots, she gave him a wry smile. "Don't even say it. These were bought for the streets of Boston, not the wilds of Maine. And, as I discovered last night, the two do not mix. I'll be better prepared on my next trip."

"Well, be careful in the meantime. Falling on ice can have nasty, long-term results. I have a bad knee to prove it."

Once in her car, Morgan took her time maneuvering out of Aunt Jo's driveway and then turned onto the main road, keeping Grant's truck in sight. He headed back toward Seaside and into the town, turning down a side street not too far from the church she'd attended that morning. When he pulled into the drive of a small, colonial-style house with dark green shutters, she eased in behind him. Even before she'd set her brake and gathered up her purse, he was opening her door.

"Looks like Bill cleared off the walk pretty well, but take my arm just in case there are any hidden patches of ice," Grant said as Morgan stepped out.

She did as he asked, and as they made their

way toward the front door she turned to him. "Did you say there would be eight people here today?"

"That's right. Kit, her husband, Bill, and their twin daughters, Nancy and Nicki, who are fifteen. My dad and uncle will be here, too, and us. So it's a small group."

"Is that the whole family?"

A shaft of pain darted across his eyes, so fleeting that Morgan wondered if she might have imagined it. "Pretty much," he replied.

So he had no family of his own, Morgan concluded. She hadn't noticed a wedding band on his hand, but that didn't always mean anything. Not all men wore rings. And it didn't matter, anyway. She had no interest in him in that way. It was clear they led very different lives and had very different philosophies. But many women would find an attractive, eligible man like Grant appealing. So why was he single?

Morgan's musings were cut short when Grant pressed the bell at the front door and it was opened seconds later by a man with dark hair touched with silver at the temples. It was the same man who had conducted the services that morning at church, she realized in surprise. From the pulpit, he'd struck her as a kind person. Up close, her impression was verified. The fine lines on his face spoke of compassion and caring, and his hazel eyes radiated warmth and welcome.

"Hi, Bill," Grant greeted him. "This is Morgan Williams. Morgan, my brother-in-law, Bill Adams."

The man held out his hand. "Welcome, Morgan."

She returned his handshake. "Thank you. I enjoyed your sermon this morning, Reverend."

"Just make it Bill. We don't stand on formalities around here. But I appreciate the kind words. Come in, both of you, before you freeze out there."

Grant ushered Morgan inside, and a petite, raven-haired woman with lively brown eyes and a warm smile hurried down the hall from the back of the house. "You must be Morgan," she said, holding out both hands. "I'm Kit. Welcome. I'm glad we persuaded you to join us today. Serenity Point is wonderful, but holidays are meant to be spent with other people."

Two older gentlemen joined them from the adjacent living room. They both shared Grant's vivid blue eyes, but there the resemblance faded. One of the men was tall and spare, though not quite as tall as Grant. He had thinning gray hair and a work-worn face with kind eyes. The other man was a couple of inches shorter and a bit heavier, with a thick head of silver hair and ruddy cheeks.

Grant drew Morgan toward them, a hand in the small of her back. "Morgan, this is my father, Andrew, and my uncle, Pete."

They reached for her hand in turn.

"Welcome," Grant's father said.

"Thank you, Mr. Kincaid."

"Just make it Andrew and Pete," he told her. "Otherwise, this place will be drowning in Mr. Kincaids. And I'd like to offer my condolences on the loss of your aunt. Jo was a fine lady. We were all real sorry to hear of her passing."

"Thank you."

"Where are the twins?" Grant asked.

"Upstairs, trying on their new clothes. Speaking of clothes, let us take your coats."

Bill reached for Morgan's coat as she slipped it off her shoulders, while Grant shrugged out of his and handed it to Kit. She reached up to give him a hug, and Morgan couldn't help overhearing their brief, muted conversation.

"Did you stop in to see Christine?" Kit asked.

"Yes."

"Did you give her our love?"

"Of course."

Morgan glanced toward them just in time to

see Kit lay her hand on Grant's shoulder while the brother and sister exchanged a look that Morgan couldn't even begin to fathom. All she knew was that she felt as if she'd witnessed some very personal exchange. Feeling like an eavesdropper, she turned away and made an innocuous comment to Andrew about the weather.

When they moved into the living room, Grant excused himself so he could change into more casual clothing. And as Morgan's gaze followed his retreating form, lingering on his broad shoulders, she couldn't help wondering: who was Christine?

"Okay, Bill, I think we're ready."

As Kit reached for her husband's hand, the other seven people around the table followed her example. Morgan found her hand taken on one side by Andrew, whose fingers were lean and sinewy, and on the other side by Grant, whose grip was firm, yet gentle—a combination she found very appealing.

Bill bowed his head. "Lord, we thank You for the gifts of family, friendship and food we enjoy this Christmas Day. We appreciate the many blessings You give us today, and every day. As we reflect on Your humble birth and

Your great example of selfless love, let us come to know and live Your message every day of our lives so that others may see, and believe. We ask You to bless all those who are alone and lonely on this day, and to let them feel Your presence in a special way. And finally, we ask You to bless those who can't be with us today in body, but who are always in our hearts. Amen."

Grant released her hand, and Morgan found herself missing the comfort of his warm clasp. Which was odd, considering she'd just met the man. But she didn't have time to dwell on her disconcerting reaction, because the conversation was boisterous and non-stop throughout the meal, filled with laughter and good-natured teasing. The bubbly twins, who had inherited their mother's raven hair and bright, animated eyes, added to the liveliness, and Morgan found herself relaxing. She even forgot about work—until her pager began to vibrate.

She reached for it and gave the message a discreet look, noting that it was from Clark. One of her clients had come up with some brilliant idea for a new ad campaign, which in his opinion couldn't wait until tomorrow. He expected Morgan to return his call today.

Placing her napkin on the table, she rose.

"I'm sorry, will you excuse me for a moment? I need to return a page."

The table fell silent, and Kit looked at her in alarm. "Is there an emergency?"

"Only in the eyes of my client."

"You mean someone wants you to return a business call *today?*" Kit asked in shock.

Morgan glanced around the table. Everyone looked dumbfounded—except Grant, who didn't appear at all surprised, just disapproving. Morgan felt a flush creep across her cheeks. These sorts of interruptions, day or night, holiday or weekend, were so much a part of her life that she took them for granted. But it was clear that this family considered it appalling that anyone would bother her on Christmas Day.

"Yes," she replied to Kit. "It's pretty much expected in the ad business that you'll be available twenty-four-seven. I'm sorry to disrupt the meal. Please go ahead. I'll be right back."

In fact, by the time Morgan dealt with her demanding client and returned to the table, almost everyone had finished eating. As she slid into her place, Kit rose.

"I put your plate in the oven, Morgan. Let me get it for you," she said.

Cold food was another thing Morgan had gotten used to over the years. Her meals were always being interrupted. "You didn't have to do that," she apologized. "And I don't want to hold things up. It looks like you're about ready for dessert."

As Kit disappeared through the door into the kitchen, Bill spoke. "It's Christmas. We have no other plans for the day, so you're not keeping us from anything. And we need to let our food settle a bit, anyway."

Although Morgan was touched by the graciousness of her hosts, she made short work of her remaining food when Kit placed the plate in front of her. Then they moved on to the cheesecake, which was every bit as good as Grant has promised. After the last bite, Morgan leaned back, her face content as she sipped her coffee.

"Wasn't this better than tuna and cold soup?"

At Grant's quiet question, Morgan turned to find him watching her, a smile playing at the corners of his mouth. Her own lips curved up in response. "Eminently."

"How about some music?" Kit said from across the table.

"Will you play, Uncle Grant?" Nancy asked.

"I'm a bit out of practice."

"You always say that," Nicki scoffed. "Besides, it won't feel like Christmas unless you play."

"In that case, how can I refuse?"

They all moved into the living room, and Morgan watched, intrigued, as Grant slid onto the bench of an upright piano and ran his fingers over the keys. For some reasons, she wouldn't have expected him to be musical. But as the family gathered around and he began to play the familiar holiday carols, she discovered that he was, in fact, quite talented. Morgan hung back, feeling a bit like an intruder in this family scene, but Kit drew her forward.

"We may not be the Metropolitan Opera chorus, but what we lack in ability we make up for in enthusiasm," she said with a laugh.

As Grant played one carol after another, Morgan found herself staring at his hands. His fingers were strong and capable, lean and long, as they moved with confidence over the ivory keys. He had wonderful hands, she realized. And all at once she found herself wondering what it would be like to be touched by them.

Trying to force her mind in a more appropriate direction, Morgan turned away from Grant and looked over the family gathered at the piano—only to be transported back to another time, another piano, another family raising sometimes off-key voices in song. Her throat constricted with emotion, and her voice faltered on the words of a familiar carol as her eyes grew misty. When Grant sent her a questioning look, her cheeks warmed and she pointed to her pager, then quickly slipped away on the pretense of returning another call.

Once in the hall, she drew a few long, deep breaths. For some reason, this day had been an emotional roller coaster, from her conversation with her sisters this morning, to her unexpected tears in church, to her wandering thoughts when she'd tried to work earlier at the cottage. The memories had been relentlessly lapping at her consciousness, much as the surf lapped against the shore at Aunt Jo's cottage. Happy memories, for the most part, but memories of days long past. Most of the time she kept them deep in her heart. But today, they had risen to the surface, throwing her off balance.

By the time Morgan returned to the living room, she had her emotions back under control. Most of the group seemed to accept her excuse for stepping away, but something in Grant's expression told her that she hadn't fooled him. His eyes were probing, questioning, curious, as if he was trying to reconcile her emotional reaction just now with the image she presented to the world of a savvy, businesslike, sophisticated career woman.

Morgan looked away before his searching gaze went too deep, before he delved right to her soul and found out things about her that even she didn't know. Things she didn't *want* to know. And suddenly she felt an overpowering need to escape. There was something about Grant Kincaid that threatened her peace of mind. As soon as she could, she thanked her hosts and said her goodbyes, explaining that after her long drive yesterday, she was ready to call it a night.

Grant insisted on walking her to her car, and short of being rude, she couldn't refuse. He took her arm as they stepped into the frigid air, and their breath formed frosty clouds in the clear, dark sky as they made their way in silence down the driveway. She fitted her key in the car lock, then turned to him, grateful for the dim light that made it hard to read expressions. "Thank you again, Grant. I had a wonderful time."

"It was our pleasure. Are we still on for Monday?"

"Yes. How about eight?"

"That's fine. I'll see you then. Drive safe."

After she slipped into her car, he shut the door behind her, watching as she backed out of the driveway. When she reached the corner, she glanced in her rearview mirror and was surprised to find Grant still standing there, his hands in the pockets of his overcoat, staring after her.

As Morgan retraced the route to the cottage, she found herself reliving her unexpected holiday dinner and thinking about Grant. She pictured his strong, competent fingers on the piano keys. Recalled the feeling of security that had swept over her when he'd taken her hand in his for the blessing. Remembered the way his smile had warmed his eyes and lit up his face.

And wondered yet again: who was Christine?

Chapter Four

❦

"Anybody home?" Grant called as he opened the door of the house he'd grown up in, the house his father and uncle now shared.

"We're in the kitchen, son," his father responded, his voice muffled.

Grant made his way down the hall and found his father and uncle wolfing down what looked like remnants from yesterday's Christmas dinner.

"Pull up a chair," Uncle Pete invited. "There's plenty. Kit made us take all this home. Said she had way too much left over. We didn't argue a whole lot."

After draping his sheepskin-lined jacket over the back of a chair and retrieving a plate from the cabinet, Grant joined the older men at the sturdy oak table.

"On your way to see Christine?" his father asked.

"Mm-hmm."

"I admire your commitment, son. But I worry about you," he said, his face troubled. "It's been two-and-a-half years, and you almost never miss a day. You're going to wear yourself out."

"I have to go, Dad. She'd do the same for me."

"I'm not saying you shouldn't go. Maybe just not every day."

Because it doesn't seem to make any difference.

The words were unspoken, but they hung in the air. His family had long ago accepted that Christine would probably never recover from the head injury that had sent her into a deep coma. Yet according to the doctors, there was brain activity. So she was still there, trapped in a broken body. Grant couldn't abandon her, even though only a tiny glimmer of hope remained in his own heart. But even if that last glimmer was finally extinguished, he still had an obligation to her. And he would see it through…for as long as she needed him.

Grant reached for a slice of prime rib and answered the way he always did. "I'll see, Dad. For now, this is what I need to do."

Pete looked at Andrew, then changed the subject. "That was one fine meal yesterday. And the leftovers aren't bad, either."

"I'm glad you convinced Jo's niece to join us, Grant." Andrew picked up Pete's cue. "Didn't sound like she had much of a meal planned. And nobody should be alone on Christmas."

"To be honest, she turned me down at first. So I called Kit, and her powers of persuasion did the trick."

Pete chuckled. "Your sister could charm a moose out of his antlers."

Grant grinned. "I agree."

"I hope Morgan had a good time," Andrew said. "Seems like that job of hers doesn't give her a minute of peace."

"I expect it's the kind of life she wants," Grant said with a shrug.

"Can't imagine why. Seems like too much stress to me. She is one high-strung young woman."

"She's a looker, though," Uncle Pete added.

"She is that," Andrew agreed. "But I feel sorry for her, living on the edge like that. Can't even enjoy a holiday without interruption."

"Don't waste your sympathy, Dad. She chose that life, so it must suit her. Just like it did Mom. In fact, she reminds me a lot of Mom."

Andrew tilted his head, his expression quizzical. "Is that right? She seems real different to me."

"How do you figure that?" Grant helped himself to some potatoes. "She's ambitious, driven, puts her career first…it's Mom all over again."

"I don't think so. There's more to Morgan Williams than that. I picked up a sort of…restlessness…like she's still searching for her path. Your mother was single-minded once she made up her mind to go for the gold. I don't get the same vibes from Morgan."

"Then you must be on the wrong wavelength," Grant said, giving him a wry look. "What do you think, Uncle Pete?"

"Like I said, she's a looker."

"You have a one-track mind, you know that?" Grant told him with a grin.

"Well, it's true."

"I didn't say it wasn't. But we weren't discussing her appearance."

"You can discuss anything you like. But when the good Lord sends a pretty woman my way, I intend to enjoy it instead of trying to psychoanalyze her."

"How did you stay a bachelor all these years?" Grant asked, shaking his head.

"I like my independence. But I don't mind lookin'."

"You're incorrigible."

"That's a fact," Pete agreed good-naturedly.

As his father and uncle began debating the merits of cherry versus maple for an upcoming project, Grant finished his lunch. Then he rose and snagged his coat off the back of his chair. "I've got to run. See you both tomorrow."

"Take care, son."

The two older men watched Grant leave, then turned their attention to the leftover cheesecake. As Andrew cut them each a generous wedge, Uncle Pete spoke.

"I worry about that boy."

"So do I."

"Livin' the way he does isn't healthy. He spends all his time at the shop or running back and forth to Brunswick to see Christine. He's got to be lonely."

"He has us. And Kit's family."

Uncle Pete brushed that aside. "You know what I mean."

"Yeah, I know," Andrew said with a sigh. "But he loved Christine, Pete. He still does. And he won't go on with his life as long as he feels she needs him."

"Sometimes it sure is hard to figure why the

good Lord gave him such a cross to bear," Uncle Pete declared, shaking his head.

"I don't expect we'll ever find the answer to that one."

"No, I don't suppose we will. But it sure does seem a waste. He's a fine man with a fine heart. He should be going home to a wife and a family every day, not spending time in that depressing extended-care facility."

"I agree," Andrew said. "We just have to pray and trust that the Lord will resolve this situation in His own way and in His own time."

"You're right," Uncle Pete conceded. "But sometimes I wish He'd just get on with it."

The jarring jangle of the phone woke Grant instantly, and he fumbled for it in the dark as he peered at the face of the digital clock beside his bed. Two-thirty in the morning. He squinted at the caller ID, and a surge of adrenaline shot through him at the familiar number. It was the extended-care facility in Brunswick.

"Hello?"

"Mr. Kincaid?"

"Yes. I have caller ID. What's the problem?" he said tersely.

"This is Walter Jackson. I'm the physician on call this evening. I'm sorry to tell you that your wife appears to have suffered a stroke. We did an initial evaluation here, but we're having her airlifted to Portland for more extensive testing."

Grant felt as if someone had kicked him in the gut, and for a moment he couldn't breathe. Christine's condition had been the same as always when he'd visited the previous afternoon after eating lunch with his dad and Uncle Pete. There'd been no indication of any problem. His grip on the phone tightened, turning his knuckles white. When he spoke, his voice was taut with tension. "How bad is it?"

"Her vitals are still relatively stable, but there has been a significant change in brain activity. Until more testing is done, I'm afraid that's all the information we have."

The man was dancing around the real issue, so Grant voiced the blunt, unspoken question that hung between them, steeling himself for the response. "Doctor, is this a life-threatening situation?"

There was a telling pause before the man responded. "It could be."

Closing his eyes, Grant sucked in a deep breath. "Okay. I'm on my way."

As he pulled on his jeans and threw on a shirt, Grant placed a quick call to his father, as well as to Christine's parents, who lived in Portland. In ten minutes flat, he was in his truck and heading south at a speed far faster than was prudent on the icy roads.

Grant had made the drive to Portland countless times, especially right after the accident. But when it became apparent that Christine's coma might be of longer duration than indicated by the initial prognosis, Grant had moved her to a medical facility in Brunswick, which was much closer to home. Still, the route to the medical center in Portland was etched on his mind, and he made the drive on autopilot, all the while struggling to rein in his panic.

Please be with me, Lord, he prayed. *And with Christine. Please don't let her suffer anymore. And please give me strength to deal with whatever waits for me in Portland. I've lived in dread of this day for two-and-a-half years. Help me to cope with this situation and guide me in whatever decisions I have to make.*

Christine's parents were at the hospital when Grant arrived, and the looks on their faces as he strode into the waiting room made his stomach lurch. Stella's eyes were red-rimmed, and Marshall's skin was ashen. Grant came to an abrupt halt, and the color drained from his own face. His voice was halting when he spoke. "Is she…"

"She's still with us, son," Marshall said.

Grant closed his eyes and wiped a hand down his face. Stella came over to him, and they exchanged a long, comforting hug. They'd all been here before. And it was a place none of them had ever wanted to visit again.

"Oh, Grant, it's such a nightmare." Her voice broke on the last word.

He couldn't agree more. He drew in a deep, steadying breath, then glanced over her head toward Marshall. "What have you heard?"

"Not much. They're still doing tests. They think a clot may have caused a stroke. But now they suspect bleeding in the brain, as well. And they…they had to put her on a respirator. She was having trouble breathing on her own."

Grant stared at the older man, his eyes bleak. Like Grant, Christine's parents had never given up hope that someday their daughter would return. But for the first time, her father looked defeated. Grant felt the sting of tears, and he struggled to keep them in check. *Lord, You've been with me through all the trauma over these difficult years. Please don't desert me now, when I need Your strength more than ever,* he prayed.

He guided Stella to one of the chairs that lined the wall, and the three of them sat in silence. Christine's parents clung to each other, and now and then Stella reached for Grant's hand and gave it a squeeze. Minutes passed, then an hour. And the little group keeping vigil grew. Andrew came next, with Pete, followed soon after by Kit and Bill. No one said much. No one needed to. All that had to be communicated was transmitted by look and by touch. Occasionally a nurse would stop by to let them know that Christine was still undergoing tests and that the doctor would speak with them as soon as the results were available, but other than that no one disturbed them.

As dawn spilled in through the windows, a white-coated figure at last appeared. Grant vaulted to his feet and strode toward the man.

"Mr. Kincaid?"

"Yes."

The physician, who looked to be in his mid-forties, held out his hand. "I'm Mark Baxter. We've done an extensive evaluation on your wife and I have all the results." He surveyed the group assembled behind Grant. "We can review them in my office, if you'd like."

Grant turned to look at the people who had stood behind him and supported him day after day, month after month, since the accident, and shook his head. "This is my family, doctor. We'd all like to hear what you have to say."

The man nodded and pulled up a chair while Grant took his seat. Although Grant didn't grasp all of the medical terms or technical explanations for what had happened to Christine, he understood the most important thing. Even though her vital signs were stable, there was no brain activity and she was no longer breathing on her own.

While the doctor explained the situation, he'd made it a point to make eye contact with everyone in the group. But now, as he finished, he focused on Grant, softening his voice. "Mr. Kincaid, we can keep your wife physically alive for an indefinite period. But she isn't going to come back. So it doesn't make a lot of sense to maintain life support. However, the decision is yours."

Grant stared at him, his face a mask of shock, and for a brief instant the doctor's composure cracked. He reached out and placed a hand on Grant's shoulder, his eyes compassionate. "I'm sorry to give you this news. Your wife is a beautiful young woman. I know how hard this must be for you. I'll be here for the next couple of hours if you want to talk with me again. Just let the nurse know and she'll page me."

A jerky nod was the only response Grant could manage.

As the doctor exited, leaving silence in his wake, Grant turned to look at the people he loved. Kit was clinging to Bill's hand as she struggled to contain the tears brimming in her eyes. Bill's demeanor was concerned and caring. Andrew's face was a mask of sorrow and shock. Pete had grown pale as raw wood.

And everyone's eyes reflected one emotion that Grant didn't yet want to deal with.

Resignation.

He turned to Stella and Marshall. Stella had begun to cry, and as he watched, Christine's parents exchanged the kind of look that long-married couples use to communicate without words. Then, Marshall directed his attention to his son-in-law. "We're with you, whatever you decide," he said, his eyes steady even though his voice wasn't.

Grant scanned the other faces again. He could sense their support. But it was also clear that the decision was his alone. And he wasn't sure he was up to the task.

Anguish contorted his features, and he reached up to rake his fingers through his uncombed hair. "I need to find the chapel," he choked out.

Bill rose. "I'll ask the nurse where it is."

He returned a few minutes later and gave

Grant the directions. "Would you like some company?" he murmured.

After a brief hesitation, Grant spoke. "Yes, but give me a little time alone first."

When Grant entered the small chapel a few minutes later, he was grateful to find it empty. He sank into a pew near the front and dropped his head into his hands, desperate for solace and guidance. How could he make the decision to remove Christine's life support? How could he end the life of the woman he'd loved with such passion and absolute devotion? The woman he'd remained faithful to through the endless months and years since the accident? Yet how could he tie her to a useless body when her spirit was clearly ready to move on?

As Grant prayed, he heard someone enter the chapel and knew that Bill had joined him. Though his brother-in-law remained in the back, leaving him undisturbed, Grant found comfort in his presence, knowing that Bill—as well as the rest of his family—would stand by him no matter what decision he made. And as a minister, Bill brought an added benefit. So many times in the past few years, Grant had turned to him for spiritual guidance when the darkness had closed in around him. And Bill had always come through for him. Perhaps he would do the same today.

Taking a deep breath, Grant turned toward his brother-in-law. Bill took that as a signal to move forward, and he made his way down the aisle to slide into the pew beside Grant.

"I don't know what to do," Grant said, his face haggard, his eyes anguished.

"It's not an easy decision," Bill acknowledged.

"I know it sounds selfish, but if I let her go, that part of my life is over forever." His voice broke on the last word.

Bill's eyes filled with compassion. "I think it's over anyway, Grant," he said, his voice gentle.

Grant closed his eyes, and a spasm of pain contorted his face. "I know," he whispered, looking up at the cross over the altar. When he spoke again, his voice was pensive. "It's odd, really. I guess you could say, in a way, that this is the answer to my prayers."

"What do you mean?"

"For the past few months, I've been asking the Lord to either take Christine home or give her back to me. But I didn't think He was going to leave the final decision in my hands." Grant turned to Bill. "I want to do the right thing. I want to abide by God's will. But I don't know the rules of this game. What am I *supposed* to do?"

"God has great respect for life, Grant. But in every way except for her physical body, Christine is gone. Only artificial means can keep her alive. In a case like this, I think God would want us to release her so that she can go home. To Him."

Grant knew that Bill was right. In his heart, he'd known it all along. The decision was straightforward. But that didn't mean it was easier to make. He bowed his head, fighting back tears. After a few seconds, he felt Bill's hand on his shoulder.

"You don't have to decide today, Grant."

"It's not…" His voice broke once more, and he tried again. "It's not going to get any easier." He wiped his sleeve across his eyes. "There's no reason to wait. It will just prolong the agony for everyone. I—I'll let the doctor know."

"Would you like to take a moment to pray first?" At Grant's nod, Bill bowed his head and placed his hand on the younger man's shoulder. "Lord, we ask You for Your sustaining strength in the days ahead as we prepare to make this difficult, final journey, and to say goodbye. We commend Christine now to Your loving care as we release her from the constraints of this earthly life, confident in Your promise that eye has not seen, ear has not heard, what God has prepared for those who love Him. We know Christine was Your loving and faithful daughter. Welcome her home now, to her eternal reward. And give comfort and strength to those of us left behind, so that we can continue to live Your word as we prepare for the day when we, too, will be called home to join those we love in the joy of Your presence."

For a long moment the two men sat in silence, but at last Grant stood. "Let's find the doctor."

They spoke with the physician first, then returned to the waiting room. One look at their grim expressions was all it took for those gathered to discern Grant's decision. Stella's face crumpled and she groped for Marshall's hand, Andrew stood and embraced his son, Pete pulled out his handkerchief and blew his nose, and Kit let the tears stream, unchecked, down her face.

They all took turns paying a final visit to Christine. Grant went last, and as he stood on the threshold of her room, the full impact of his decision began to register. For two-and-a-half years, he'd planned his life around his visits to his wife. Now that life was coming to an end. This was his last visit.

Grant moved into the room and made his

way to the side of the bed. Christine's face was partially obscured by the respirator, her chest rising and falling to its mechanical rhythm. With distaste, he scanned the complicated machinery and equipment that surrounded her, keeping her body alive. He knew this wasn't what she would have wanted. The woman he married had had sparkle and vibrancy and enthusiasm. She had been more alive than anyone he'd ever met, embracing each day with joy and anticipation. Trapping her in a useless body when everything else that defined her was already gone would be wrong. And despite his grief, a sudden peace settled over him.

He reached for her cool hand, then sat on the bed beside her. "I've come to say goodbye, Christine," he said, his voice ragged. "I hope somehow you know what's in my heart, even if you can't hear me. Because the love I feel for you has never dimmed. And it never will. When you leave, you'll take a part of me with you. The part that is yours for always." He searched her face, and the anguish in his eyes was as searing as a white-hot poker laid against bare skin. When he spoke again, his voice was raw with pain. "Dear God, I wish things could have been different! I wish you had recovered, and we could have lived the life we looked forward to with such joy. I wish we could have raised the children we wanted, and grown old together to enjoy our grandchildren. But that wasn't in God's plan for us. I don't understand why this happened. I never will. But I've tried very hard to accept it, and to be grateful for the brief time we had together. It was a blessing I'll cherish all of my life."

He leaned over and kissed her forehead, then reached up with trembling fingers to brush the hair back from her face. "Goodbye, my love," he whispered. "Rest in peace now. And never forget how much I love you."

Grant stood, grasping a piece of equipment for support when his legs threatened to buckle. For a full minute, he stared down at Christine's face, the image blurring as tears ran down his face. Finally he forced himself to walk toward the door.

As he reached for the handle he turned, allowing himself one last moment alone with his wife. One last moment to recall the joy he'd known with this special woman. Then calling up every ounce of his courage, he opened the doors and motioned to the waiting nurse.

Concern furrowing her brow, Morgan glanced again at the clock. Eight-thirty. Though she had only known him a short time, Grant didn't strike her as the type to be late for a meeting. Not without calling to explain.

Pulling out her Blackberry, she searched for his home number, then punched it in. But after three rings, his answering machine kicked in. She called his work number next, surprised to discover it was a cabinet shop. Kincaid Woodworks. There'd been little talk of business on Christmas, but she did recall Grant's father mentioning something about a shipment of lumber. It hadn't registered until now. So Kincaid Woodworks must be a family business. And Grant must be a carpenter. Interesting. She'd just assumed he had some sort of office job.

But that didn't matter now, she reminded herself. If Grant wasn't going to show, she needed to get back to Boston.

Maybe Kit would know where he was, she speculated, retrieving the tiny Seaside phone book she'd noticed in the kitchen. But again, she got an answering machine. This time, though, she left a message.

As she hung up, Morgan decided to give Grant until nine. Then she was out of here.

In the end, she gave him until nine-thirty. Finally, her patience exhausted, she packed up her car and headed back to Boston.

Half an hour later, as she pulled onto the highway for the long drive south, she tried to concentrate on the ad campaign that had interrupted her holiday meal. She needed to have some ideas ready to present to the client by Wednesday.

But though she gave it a mighty effort, she couldn't focus.

Because something back in Seaside just didn't feel right

"Morgan? It's Kit Adams."

A tingle of alarm raced along Morgan's spine, and she tightened her grip on the receiver. She remembered Kit's voice as lilting and upbeat, but the woman on the other end of the line sounded shaky and tearful.

"Is something wrong?"

"I got your message. And Grant sends his apologies for missing your meeting. But we…we've had a death in the family." Her voice was so choked she had trouble speaking.

"I'm so sorry," Morgan said, thinking of Grant's father and uncle. But they'd both seemed in good health. "Was it someone…close?"

"Very. Grant's wife, Christine, suffered a massive stroke on Sunday night. It left her…brain dead…and unable to breathe on her own…so

Grant made the decision to…to discontinue life support." Kit's voice caught on a sob.

Morgan stared at the bleak, gray Boston sky outside her window, her face a mask of shock as she tried to assimilate Kit's news. "I'm so sorry. I…I didn't even know Grant was married."

Kit sniffled. "For six years. Two and a half years ago, while they were on a hiking vacation, Christine fell and suffered a head injury. She's been in a coma ever since."

Morgan closed her eyes. "I had no idea," she whispered.

"Most of us gave up hope of her recovery a long time ago," Kit said, her voice still unsteady. "But Grant never did. He visited her every day. I think he always believed that one day he'd walk in and find her awake, waiting for him. But it…it never happened. And now the Lord has called her home. Even though most of us expected it to happen at some point, it's still such a shock."

"Is there anything I can do?" Morgan asked, feeling helpless.

"Just pray for him," Kit said tearfully. "Because as hard as the past two and a half years have been for him, saying goodbye will be even worse."

Chapter Five

~❦~

Morgan turned up the collar of her coat as a gust of icy wind lashed at her body, making the struggle across the uneven ground at the cemetery more difficult. She supposed she could have remained at the church, as many had, while the family and close friends concluded the funeral rite with the final commendation to the grave. After all, she didn't fall into either of those categories. And maybe she shouldn't even have come. Maybe she was infringing on what was intended to be a very private service.

But she'd wanted to be here, for the whole thing—even if it did mean taking a day off work. Though she and Grant might be very different, connected only by chance through an unexpected gift from Aunt Jo, she wanted to let him know, by her presence, that she cared. And that she grieved for his loss.

Morgan's thin gloves didn't offer much protection from the biting wind, so she shoved her hands into the pockets of her coat. While she waited for the final, brief service to begin, her thoughts turned to the woman Grant had loved. After speaking with family and friends last night at the visitation, and listening to the eulogies today, it was clear that Christine had been a very special woman. Intelligent. Talented. Loving. With a deep faith that had been the guiding force in her life.

But the accolades hadn't been only for Christine. She'd learned a lot about Grant, too, as family and friends had praised his steadfast loyalty, his faithfulness and his unwavering devotion. Morgan couldn't even begin to comprehend the overwhelming sense of loss he must be feeling. She only hoped that the tremendous outpouring of love and support he'd received over the past couple of days, and the overflowing crowd at the church, had offered him some comfort.

Bill took his place beside the casket, and motioned everyone to move closer. Morgan complied, but still remained somewhat in the background. Grant and Kit sat in front, their hands entwined. Andrew was on the other side of Grant, his hand resting on his son's knee. Pete was up front, too, of course, as were Kit's twins. So were Christine's parents, whom she'd met the night before.

And Grant's mother was there, as well. She'd arrived last night, too late to visit the funeral home, so Morgan hadn't met her. But she'd overheard someone at church point her out to a friend. From various conversations, she'd discovered that Grant's parents were separated, that his mother had a prestigious job in Boston with a big-name financial firm, and that she was somewhat estranged from the family.

As everyone settled into place and Bill began the brief graveside service, Morgan sent Grant's mother a curious glance. Her fashionable clothing was elegant rather than trendy, and her hair and makeup were perfect. She sat at the far end of the front row, and Morgan noted that she glanced at her watch several times while Bill spoke.

As the service ended, Morgan's gaze shifted back to Grant. He stood, shook Bill's hand, then turned to greet those who moved forward to speak with him. Again, Morgan felt out of place and moved a few steps farther away. She'd given him her condolences last night; she didn't need to intrude on this final, private moment.

Slowly, people began to drift back toward their cars, leaving just the immediate family around the casket. As Morgan turned to go, as well, she caught sight of Grant's mother, standing off to one side. She watched as the woman checked her pager, then turned her back on the group gathered at the grave site and withdrew her cell phone from her purse. After punching in a number, she put the phone to her ear.

With a jolt, Morgan recognized herself. She'd done something very similar at Aunt Jo's funeral. It was obvious that, like Morgan, Grant's mother was a workaholic. While her son was saying his final goodbye to his wife, she was on her cell phone taking care of business instead of comforting him.

Morgan suddenly felt sick to her stomach.

She turned away sharply, almost as if she'd been slapped, and stumbled toward her car, pausing just once to glance back. Bill and Grant were the only ones left at the grave site now, and the minister had his arm around Grant's shoulders. Grant's head was bowed, and his hand rested on the coffin. He nodded at something Bill said, then the minister turned away, leaving Grant alone with his pain.

Morgan's heart contracted, and she felt an unexpected, overpowering urge to go to him, to touch him, to ease his sense of loss, to let him know he wasn't alone. But that wasn't within her power. Nor was it her place.

So she turned away, leaving him to his final, private moment of wrenching grief. And as she got into her car, it occurred to her how very lucky Christine had been to be loved by a man like Grant. Maybe he wasn't successful in the worldly sense. Maybe he didn't have a high-powered job and make an executive's salary. But as she'd learned in the past few days, he had other compensations in his life. Like love. And family. And faith.

And she'd learned something else, as well. Grant Kincaid was a kind, decent, faithful man who had deeply loved his wife and lived the vows he'd taken on his wedding day long after most would have collapsed under the burden and relinquished their responsibilities.

As strange as it seemed, Morgan found herself envying a dead woman. Because even though Christine's life with Grant had been brief, it was clear that it had been full and happy, based on a profound, abiding love that transcended even death.

The kind of love Morgan had never known.

And all at once her eyes flooded with tears.

For Grant's loss.

And for her own.

"Morgan, there's a Grant Kincaid out front for you. He doesn't have an appointment, but he's a hottie! I figured I'd check with you before I told him to get lost."

Startled, Morgan looked up at the receptionist, the ad layouts strewn on her desk forgotten. After the funeral, Morgan hadn't expected to see Grant again until the Good Shepherd board meeting in Portland in January. What had brought him to Boston? And, more specifically, to her office?

"Go ahead and send him back, Lauren," Morgan said.

"Sure thing. Let me know if you need me to take notes or anything," she said with a wink.

When Grant appeared in her office door a couple of minutes later, Morgan had to agree with Lauren. Despite the weariness in his face, and the sadness that lurked in the depths of his eyes, Grant Kincaid was a man who could make women's heads turn.

He was dressed in a sheepskin-lined jacket and worn jeans that hugged his lean hips. His hair was a bit windblown and his eyes were an intense blue in the midday sun that streamed in her large office window, which offered a panoramic view of the Boston skyline. Her gaze dropped to the hands that had mesmerized her on Christmas before she forced it back to his face.

She stood and held out her hand. "Good morning, Grant. Come in."

He returned her greeting, his grip sure and firm. "Sorry for the unexpected visit, but I had to come to Boston to take some measurements for a new commission and I thought I'd drop off some additional Good Shepherd material. I planned to give it to you when we met after Christmas, but..." A shaft of pain ricocheted through his eyes, and he cleared his throat. "Anyway, I was in the neighborhood, and with the board meeting coming up, I figured I'd just deliver it in person." He held out a large manila envelope.

"I'll be sure to review it before the meeting," she promised, setting it on her credenza. "Can I offer you a cup of coffee?"

"I don't want to keep you from your work." He surveyed her cluttered desk.

"It'll wait. Have a seat." She punched the button for the intercom. "Lauren, could you bring my visitor a cup of coffee?" She settled into her chair and turned her attention back to Grant. "So, how are you doing?"

"Okay, I guess. I'm just trying to take it a day at a time right now. Thank you again for coming for the funeral. I didn't expect that. I know it's a long trip."

"I wanted to be there. For myself. And maybe to represent Aunt Jo. You and she must have been great friends."

"Yes, we were. I met her at church when I was eleven, right after my parents separated, and she became sort of a mother figure to me. So I knew her for more than a quarter of a century. For the past fifteen years, I've handled all of the maintenance and upkeep at Serenity Point."

Lauren interrupted then with the coffee, lingering as long as possible. When she finally left, Morgan spoke again.

"I noticed how well cared for the place is. And the furnishings in the cottage are beautiful. There's a lot of original art, and some of the wood furniture is gorgeous."

"Jo believed in supporting local artists and craftspeople, and my family benefited from that philosophy. My father made the bookcase by the window in the living room, and my uncle made the rocking chair."

"I'm impressed. What about the secretary?" She'd noticed that piece in particular, with its intricate carving and mullioned glass doors.

"That's one of mine."

"Now I'm even more impressed. It's beautiful." She reached for a pen and played with it, her face thoughtful. "You know, I had no idea what your profession was until I called your shop the day of our meeting. I was…surprised…when I found out you were a carpenter."

Grant stiffened. He knew what that look on her face meant. *Can't you do better?* He'd seen it before, on occasion, and it used to make him feel compelled to defend his choice of profession. But not anymore. He was fine with his life's work, and if others weren't, that was their problem. So he gave his standard answer to her reaction. "Yes. Just like the greatest man that ever lived," he said with quiet conviction.

His withdrawal was palpable, and Morgan knew that she had offended him. Which had in no way been her intent. But she supposed her response could have been interpreted as snobbish. In her circle, people who worked with their hands were somehow held in lower esteem than the people who carried cell phones and pagers and had power lunches every day. After all, the "white-shirt" crowd was doing important things. Things that mattered.

Like creating fleeting ad campaigns for toothpaste, she thought, sparing the layout in front of her a quick glance.

By contrast, the beautiful secretary created by Grant was a work of art, destined to be a treasured heirloom that would be passed from generation to generation.

Suddenly she felt ashamed.

"I'm sorry, Grant," she said, her voice contrite. "That didn't come out quite right. My own father worked with his hands. In a different way, though. He was a simple farmer who loved the land. A good man, who worked too hard and died too young."

A wave of melancholy washed over her, and her eyes grew sad. Her dad had been a good father. But she'd seen what heartache—and hardship—and an unstable profession that depended on the vagaries of the weather could do to a person. She'd wanted a more forgiving career for herself, one that offered security and steady income, as well as the luxuries that she'd never known growing up. She had those now. Yet something still seemed to be missing. Something she hadn't yet defined—on purpose—because somehow she sensed that it represented a threat to the life she'd constructed with such care and singular focus. And that scared her.

Realizing that the silence had lengthened,

she continued. "Anyway, I had the greatest respect for him and his choice of career. We all have to march to the beat of our own drummer."

There had been an appealing softness in Morgan's eyes when she'd spoken about her father, Grant realized. And for just an instant he'd glimpsed in her what his father had commented on once—a sense of yearning, or perhaps searching. As if the life she had chosen was perhaps not the one that best suited her—and she knew it. Not on a conscious level, perhaps. But somewhere deep inside.

"No offense taken," he assured her.

She gave him a grateful smile. "Good. Then tell me more about Good Shepherd Camp. And how Aunt Jo got involved."

"I can take the credit—or the blame—for that."

"How so? When I talked to Mary, she said Aunt Jo had been involved for many years. Long before you were an adult."

"That's right. As I said, when I first met Jo, my parents had just separated. I was pretty angry at the world, and I'd started to get into some minor trouble at school. Jo not only took me under her wing, but found Good Shepherd for me. If you've read the material I sent earlier, you know it's a Christian camp for troubled children. She thought it would be a good environment for me and, as usual, she was right. It gave me a new perspective and helped me establish a solid foundation for my faith. I went every summer until I was sixteen, and then worked for a number of years while I was in school as a counselor. I still volunteer as a counselor one week each summer."

"But now there are problems with the camp?"

"Yes. Our operating costs are continuing to climb and donations no longer cover our expenses. So the camp is facing a severe financial crisis that could put us out of business. Yet the need for the camp is as critical now as ever. Maybe more so. I told you my story, but we have kids today who come from far worse situations than I did, who are in desperate need of guidance and a loving hand. Society has already written off some of them. But we give them another chance. For a lot of the kids, it's their last hope of a turnaround. We don't reach everybody, of course. But a significant number do respond. So we want to do everything we can to keep Good Shepherd running."

Morgan was impressed by Grant's passion for the camp, and by his determination to keep it solvent. Most of the people of her acquaintance only got excited about things that offered some sort of pay-off. The old what's-in-it-for-me routine. But Grant really cared about this cause. Even though he'd paid off his own debt to the camp long ago, he was still committed to supporting it because it might help other people. It reminded her of the way her sister, A.J., operated. She was always more concerned with helping others than helping herself, an attitude that had cost her— in more ways than one. And Morgan was sure it had cost Grant in ways he hadn't articulated.

"Well, I'll do my best to help," she promised.

"That's all we ask." He dug into the pocket of his jeans and withdrew a folded piece of paper. "I've jotted down the board meeting dates through May. Mary will send you more detailed information and the agendas. But I wanted you to have these so you can incorporate them into your schedule. As you know, we meet at the headquarters, in Portland."

Scanning the list Grant handed her, Morgan noted that all of the meetings were on Saturday—which was almost always a workday for her. And Portland was a long way from Boston. At least it was only for five months, she consoled herself.

As if reading her mind, Grant spoke. "We'll appreciate whatever help you can give us. I know this is very inconvenient for you."

"True. But I'll manage. This is far easier to deal with than Aunt Jo's other stipulation. At the rate I'm going, I'll be lucky to log a week at the cottage, let alone four, before the six months is up."

Grant took a last swallow of coffee, put the cup on the desk, then stood. "Well, I'm sure Jo put the conditions in her will for a reason. She was a very smart woman."

As Morgan said her goodbyes, she reflected on his last words. Jo *had* been a smart woman. But she hadn't exactly made it easy for any of her nieces to claim their bequests. Morgan in particular. Yet Grant seemed convinced that she'd had her reasons. And maybe she had.

But Morgan didn't have a clue what they were.

Chapter Six

~❧~

"Oh, Grant, come in! You have to see what just arrived!"

Grant stepped into the foyer of Kit's house and smiled at his sister. "Whatever it is, it must be good. Your face is lit up like a Christmas tree."

She took his hand, led him into the dining room and pointed to the table, where a huge arrangement of tropical flowers occupied the place of honor in the center.

Grant stared at the overflowing basket. "Wow!"

"My sentiments exactly. Come and look." She pulled him into the room and began pointing out the exotic blossoms. "Protea, birds of paradise, orchids, ginger, more orchids...I feel like I've been transported to the tropics!"

Bill was always good about sending Kit flowers on their anniversary, but that was two months off. And her birthday wasn't until June. Besides, he never ordered anything as extravagant as this. Grant turned to her with a puzzled look. "So who sent them?"

"Morgan! It's a thank-you for Christmas."

He turned back to the flowers. He couldn't even imagine what the extravagant arrangement had cost. More than he made on a good day, no doubt.

"Can you believe she remembered one random comment I made at dinner, about how nice it would be to spend a few days somewhere warm and tropical this time of year? Listen to the note." Kit picked up a small card from the table. "'Sorry this is a bit belated, but things have been hectic here. Thank you so much for your gracious hospitality on Christmas. I can't transport you to Hawaii, but maybe this will bring a little bit of the tropics to you.' Wasn't that thoughtful?"

"It was a very nice gesture," he conceded.

Setting the note down, Kit placed her hands on her hips. "That, dear brother, is an understatement. A simple thank-you note would have been more than sufficient."

"Maybe this was easier. All she had to do was pick up the phone and place an order. It didn't take much time away from her work."

She tilted her head and studied him. "That

wasn't a very gracious comment, considering she made the trip all the way up here for—" she blinked back sudden tears "—for the funeral."

Grant felt his neck grow red. He hated being called on the carpet by his older sister. Especially when she was right. "That's true. It wasn't," he admitted.

"So what gives with you and Morgan? She seems like a nice enough woman. Why don't you like her?"

"I didn't say I didn't like her. We're just very different."

"So? You're only business partners, after all. And she strikes me as very efficient. I would think you'd be glad to have a partner like that."

Again, she was right. The fact that he and Morgan clashed philosophically and personally was irrelevant. Their partnership was short-term at best. He sighed and raked his fingers through his hair. "You sure don't cut a guy any slack."

Her eyes softened, and she slipped her arm around his waist. "Sorry. I know you're not yourself right now. I just think you're being too hard on her." Then she threw him her zinger. "Probably because you think she's a lot like Mom."

He shot her a startled look. "Have you been talking to Dad?"

"No. Why?"

"I just wondered. And she does remind me of Mom."

"I don't think they're anything alike," Kit declared.

His eyes grew suspicious. "Are you sure you haven't talked to Dad?"

"Did he say the same thing?"

"More or less."

"Well, I think he's right."

"How can you say that? She's driven, work-focused and has no life except her job. Nor does she seem to want one."

"How do you know?"

"I've talked with her enough to get the picture. And I know you. You're a talented graphic designer and you love your work, too. But you've got balance in your life. She doesn't."

"I'm also married. With children. It might be different if I was single."

"I doubt it. Besides, I suspect Morgan has put marriage on the back burner so she can concentrate on getting ahead in her career."

"Why do you say that?"

"Well, as Uncle Pete put it in his usual succinct style, she's a looker. She's also smart. And considerate," he added, indicating the flowers. "There must be plenty of guys who've pursued her."

"Did it ever occur to you that maybe she's just never met the right man?"

He gave her a skeptical look. "I don't think she's in the market."

"Or maybe she's divorced," Kit speculated, her tone thoughtful.

Grant frowned. That possibility had never occurred to him. And for reasons he couldn't even begin to understand, it bothered him. So he changed the subject. "Look, am I going to get that lunch you promised or not?"

Kit grinned and gave him a playful jab in the shoulder. "Changing the subject does not get you off the hook, dear brother. We'll resume this conversation another day. But in the meantime, lunch is ready."

As Grant followed her toward the kitchen, his frown deepened. Not because Kit had made it clear that she wasn't finished with this subject. But because the subject itself bothered him.

Which didn't make any sense. He and Morgan were merely business partners and her personal life should be no concern of his.

"Hey, Morgan, did you hear the news?"

Annoyed at the distraction, Morgan glanced

up from the layouts she was reviewing. David Butler, another account executive, had entered her office and closed the door behind him. And he looked worried. "No. What news?"

"The acquisition is a done deal."

Morgan felt her stomach lurch. There'd been rumors for the past few weeks that her firm was going to be acquired by a larger agency, but management had assured them that there was no immediate need for concern. So much for the firm's professed value of open, honest communication with employees. "Are you sure?"

"It just came through on e-mail. There's a meeting in an hour. What a present to come back to after the holidays," he said in disgust, shoving his hands in his pockets. "So what do you think is going to happen?"

"I don't have a clue." She wasn't that worried, though. She'd put in her time. Clark knew she was a hard worker and was committed to her job. She was less sure how David would fare. Though he was talented, he'd never put in the long hours she did or been as single-minded in his pursuit of success. He'd made time for other things in his life—which might come back to haunt him now. But she didn't point any of that out. He was worried enough as it was. "We both have highprofile accounts. If anyone is going to be safe, it should be us," she reassured him.

David didn't look convinced. "Yeah. In a perfect world that would be true. But you know what they say about the rat race. You have to be a rat to participate. And I have a feeling the rats are about to come crawling out of the woodwork."

"Let's not panic," Morgan said, though her own stomach was still fluttering with tension. "Maybe we'll find out more at the meeting."

But she didn't feel any better after the brief gathering an hour later. It was clear her own boss had no idea what was coming next. Management had simply asked people to be patient as transition details were worked out, and had assured them that there would be no immediate changes.

So Morgan didn't suspect a thing when she was called into Clark's office on Friday—until she saw a human resources representative sitting at his conference table. She came to an abrupt halt on the threshold as a sudden feeling of dread washed over her.

Clark ushered her in, then shut the door behind her. "Have a seat, Morgan. Can I get you something to drink?" There were lines of tension in his face, and his voice sounded tight.

"No, thanks."

"You know Luke Preston, don't you?"

"We've met," Morgan said, forcing her legs to carry her forward. She shook the man's hand, then sat across from him.

Clark sat at the head of the table and opened a folder that lay in front of him. "First of all, Morgan, I want you to know that your contributions to this firm have been much appreciated over the past eight years. You're dedicated and hard-working and have great potential. If things had remained the same, I think it would be safe to say that you were destined to rise very high in the ranks here.

"But, as we all know, things change. And our acquisition is going to have a tremendous impact on this firm. Much more so than we first thought. Our new owner has lost some major accounts in the past few months, and the management there has decided to assign some of its key people to our primary accounts. Many of which you handle."

He took a deep breath. "Aside from asking you to take a step back—which I would never do because I don't think it would be in your long-term best interest—we have no choice but to let you go, Morgan. However, we've worked out a nice severance package for you, which Luke will explain."

As the human resources representative began

to go over the severance pay, extension of benefits, outplacement help and myriad other things, Morgan felt as if she'd been dropped into the twilight zone. The whole experience was surreal. This wasn't how things were supposed to work. If you gave up your life, if you devoted yourself to your job, if you made sacrifices and put your own needs last, you were supposed to be rewarded. Not fired. This couldn't be happening. They couldn't do this to her! She'd been told she was a rising star. That great things were in store for her if she kept up her pace and her focus.

But it had all been a lie.

"That's pretty much it, Morgan." Luke closed the folder and slid it across the table toward her. "Do you have any questions?"

She forced her attention back to the man across from her. He was acting as if nothing was wrong, as if her life hadn't just been turned upside down, as if this was business as usual. And maybe it was, for him, she realized with a jolt.

When she didn't respond, Luke shifted uncomfortably and glanced at Clark.

"We know this is a shock, Morgan," her boss acknowledged. "And it wasn't my choice. But you'll do well wherever you go. And I'll be happy to give you a glowing recommendation."

Dazed she turned to look at him. "When is this effective?"

"Immediately. The new management wants a clean and quick change. You can stay today to pack your personal things, or you can come back over the weekend, whichever is easier for you."

"*This* is my last day?" she said, stunned. "But…I'm in the middle of several major campaigns. What about my clients?"

"They'll be reassigned." Clark looked back at Luke, then both men stood, signaling the end of the meeting. "If you have any questions as you look over that material, just give us a call next week."

Morgan slowly stood and took their hands as they wished her well. Clark led the way toward the door, and as he opened it to let her out she saw David waiting on the other side. The instant she came into view his face went several shades paler, and she saw his Adam's apple bob as he swallowed.

Morgan felt sorry for David. Unlike him, she didn't have a big mortgage, a stay-at-home spouse or two kids in expensive private schools. No wonder he looked panicked. Yet in another way, she felt more sorry for herself. Even though he was facing a crisis, David had something she didn't have. By balancing the demands of his career with his personal life, he'd managed to find time to maintain his relationship with God and create a strong home life. As a result, he now had his faith and his family to sustain him.

As Morgan made her way back to her office, numb with shock, she realized that she didn't have anything to fall back on. Her sisters were far away, and God… well, He seemed farther away still. She was on her own. And she had no idea where to go from here. She'd mapped out her future, played by the rules, done everything she was supposed to do to get ahead. She'd felt in control of her destiny.

But the rules had changed with no warning, leaving her with an obsolete game plan and robbing her of the future she'd planned with such care.

And for the first time in her life, she was afraid.

"Okay, I think we're ready to begin."

As Grant spoke, the eight people milling about the small meeting room made their way to the simple wooden conference table. Morgan hovered in the background, and Grant looked over at her with a smile. "Anywhere is fine, Morgan. We don't have assigned seats."

As she took a place at the far end of the table, Grant watched her. She'd arrived for her first Good Shepherd Camp board meeting at the last minute, and he hadn't had a chance to talk with her one on one. But he'd been startled by the change in her appearance. In the two weeks since he'd visited her office, she'd lost weight. Her fair complexion was far paler than he remembered, and the spark of energy that had radiated from her eyes had all but disappeared. He continued to observe her as she withdrew some papers from her briefcase, noting that her hands weren't quite steady. Something was very wrong, he realized.

But he didn't have time right now to dwell on Morgan's problems. He could barely manage his own grief. And there were pressing Good Shepherd issues to deal with.

"Good morning, everyone. Thanks for coming out on this cold, snowy day. Let me begin by introducing you to Morgan Williams, Jo Warren's great-niece. She's going to be serving as an advisory member of the board for the next few months as we plan our fund-raising campaign. Her extensive experience in the advertising and marketing business will be invaluable, and I know I speak for all of us when I say we're grateful for her assistance."

Grant moved on to a review of the financials for the camp, which were pretty dismal. As the board discussed the numbers in excruciating detail, Morgan zoned out. It had taken every ounce of her willpower to get up, get dressed and show up for this meeting, when all she wanted to do was crawl back in bed, pull the covers over her head and escape to the oblivion of sleep. She'd been feeling more and more like that with each passing day. Which she knew wasn't healthy.

On the other hand, she supposed she was reacting in a pretty typical fashion to the trauma that had derailed her life. She'd gone through the stereotypical emotions in rapid succession after her layoff—shock, disbelief, anger. But after a few days she'd swung into action, blanketing the Boston ad community with résumés, assuming that she'd have an offer in no time.

However, after two weeks she still hadn't had even a nibble. So, the stories she'd been reading about the tough job market must have been true, after all. At this point, she'd pretty much exhausted the Boston area. She wasn't sure what to do next.

Her self-confidence was also eroding with

dizzying speed. She'd always thought she was good at what she did. But if that was true, why weren't her skills being recognized? Didn't *anyone* in the advertising world think she had value? And if not, were they right? So much of her identity had been tied to her job that without it—her title, her office, her work—she wasn't even sure who she was anymore. And that feeling wasn't just disconcerting. It was terrifying.

"That sounds like a good idea, Sylvia. Let's ask Morgan."

Morgan heard her name and forced her thoughts back to the present. A flush spread over cheeks as she realized she'd missed a good part of the discussion. It reminded her of the few embarrassing times in grade school when she'd been caught daydreaming. "I'm sorry, I'm afraid I missed that last comment. Could you repeat it, please?"

Grant's eyes were probing, questioning, discerning. But to Morgan's surprise, his look was caring, rather than critical, which touched her, considering all he'd been through. Lines of weariness and sorrow were etched on his gaunt face, and the purple shadows under his eyes spoke of sleepless nights. Yet despite his own pain, he was still sensitive to the moods of others.

"Of course," he replied. "Sylvia was asking whether it would be a good idea to try and tap into alumni of the camp as we begin our fund-raising effort."

"That makes sense," Morgan concurred. "Is your alumni mailing list up to date?"

"As much as we can make it," Mary spoke up. "We try to stay in touch with the kids, but it's not easy. So we've lost contact with quite a few."

"Are you aware of any high-profile alumni who might be willing to go public with their support of the camp?"

"A few."

"They'll be a good resource." Morgan scanned the sheet of paper in front of her, where she'd scribbled some notes as she'd reviewed the camp material that Grant had sent. "You might want to consider some sort of black-tie fund-raising dinner and auction, as well. That type of event can be very lucrative if it's well-promoted and supported by the right people. That's even more true if you can bring in some good entertainment."

"I'm not sure we have the connections for that," Sylvia told her.

"I have some contacts I may be able to use to help pull something like this together," Morgan offered. "And I can help plan and arrange the publicity and marketing. But you also might want to think about appointing an advisory board of high-profile people who can lend their names—and support—to the camp and help to chair events like this. That's why I asked about successful alumni, but the board could consist of anyone who supports your work. I think that's critical, because even though I'm confident we can pull off an event this year and generate enough income to get the camp through another season, you need some people dedicated to fund-raising year-round on an ongoing basis. And they have to be people with the right contacts, who can get you the support you need."

"Those ideas sound good," Grant agreed. "We'll put our heads together for some potential advisory board members. And how does everyone feel about the concept of a fund-raising event of some kind?" At the murmur of assent from the board, he looked at Morgan. "I'd say that's a go. What do you think about timing on an event like this?"

"I can draw up some preliminary ideas that you could circulate to the board before the next meeting. If we can nail this down by the February meeting, I'd say we could plan an event for early May."

"Is everyone okay with that timing?" Grant asked. Again, there was a positive reaction. "Then let's move on to some other issues."

By the time the meeting adjourned a half hour later, Morgan was more than ready to head home. But before she could make a fast exit a couple of the board members cornered her to chat about the fund-raising event. Summoning up a weary smile, she did her best to seem enthusiastic about the project.

From the other side of the room, Grant glanced her way as he spoke with Sylvia, who had waylaid him as he began to make his way over to Morgan. He'd managed to put concerns about Morgan aside during the meeting, using a skill he'd honed over the past two-and-a half years. Compartmentalizing his life was the only way he'd been able to survive. But now that the meeting was over, he couldn't ignore her pallor or obvious distress. They might only be reluctant business partners, but he couldn't let her walk out of this room without at least making a few discreet inquiries and offering help if she needed it. It was the Christian thing to do.

Sylvia was still talking when Morgan began to gather up her briefcase and purse, and as she headed toward the door he laid a hand on the older woman's arm. "Excuse me, Sylvia." He looked toward the door. "Morgan!" She paused, then turned with obvious reluctance. "Could you wait a minute? I'd like to speak with you before you leave."

At first he didn't think she was going to comply, but after a brief hesitation, she nodded.

"Don't let me keep you, Grant," Sylvia said. "I was finished, anyway." The woman started toward the door, and Grant followed. When she reached Morgan, she extended her hand. "We appreciate your help, my dear. Your ideas all sound wonderful, and I'll look forward to seeing more details soon."

"Thank you."

"Talk to you soon, Grant."

They watched Sylvia leave, then Grant turned toward Morgan. Up close she looked even worse. There were faint shadows under eyes, and fine lines at their corners, as if she hadn't been sleeping. When she lifted a hand to push her hair back from her face, it was trembling, and his gut clenched. Whatever had happened to her had been bad. Really bad. And even though he had plenty of his own problems to deal with, he couldn't ignore her pain. "Could I buy you a cup of coffee before you tackle the long drive back to Boston?" he offered.

Morgan was touched—and tempted—by the unexpected offer. She could use a sympathetic ear about now. But adding to Grant's already heavy burden wouldn't be fair. So she shook her head. "Thank you, but I need to get back." She started to turn away, but again his voice stopped her.

"Look...I don't mean to pry, but...is everything okay?"

Morgan took a deep breath, then turned back to him. His eyes were so kind, so caring, so empathetic, that her composure took a dangerous dive. She needed to get out of there, she realized. Fast. Before she completely lost it and made a total fool of herself.

"Yes. I'm fine," she lied, but the tremor in her voice said otherwise. "Look, I really need to run. I'll be in touch."

And with that she fled.

Troubled, Grant watched her go. He'd given her an opening to share her problem, whatever it was, and she'd brushed him aside. There was nothing else he could do. Besides, he had enough to deal with right now. He didn't need to add Morgan Williams's dilemma, whatever it was, to his list. It would be better if he put her of his mind and focused on getting on with his life.

But he had a feeling that wasn't going to be so easy to do.

Morgan's gaze shifted from her bank statement to the figures she'd scribbled on the lined sheet of yellow legal paper in front of her, then back again. Things were not looking good.

Cradling her mug in her hands, she leaned back in her chair and took a sip of her now-lukewarm coffee as she glanced out the window. The bleak, gray, early-February Boston sky did nothing to raise her sprits.

Her severance pay was vanishing with remarkable speed as she struggled to maintain the lifestyle she'd created. She'd made good money—but she'd also spent a lot of it. It was important in her world to live a life that spelled *success* in capital letters. Everyone she knew lived this way, struggling to present an image that they hoped would breed big-time success in the future. After all, people who appeared to be successful were more likely to *be* successful. At least that had been the philosophy of her peers.

So she'd paid big bucks for a prestigious address in a very trendy section of town, even if she did have just a tiny apartment in the building, drove an expensive sports car, wore designer clothing and ate at fine restaurants. But she couldn't maintain that lifestyle much longer without a regular salary, and she'd still had no responses to her résumés. So she'd come to the conclusion that she'd have to broaden her job search beyond Boston.

In the meantime, she needed to hear a friendly voice. Meaning A.J. or Clare. Not that she wanted to burden her sisters with her problems; they were dealing with their own inheritance challenges. But at least if she talked with them she'd be reminded that there were people in the world who cared about her. Clare would be easiest to reach at this hour, so without giving herself time for second thoughts, she punched in her older sister's number.

Clare answered on the second ring, and even though Morgan did her best to sound upbeat, it took her sister less than thirty seconds to discern that there was a problem.

"So what's wrong?" she asked before they'd barely said hello.

"Who said anything was wrong?"

"You didn't have to. I lived with you for years, remember? I know how to read your moods. Is it something with the job?"

"I guess you could say that." Morgan took a deep breath. "I don't have it anymore."

For a moment, there was silence. When Clare spoke again, her voice was laced with concern. "What happened, Morgan?"

Morgan gave her the bad news. "I've been looking for something else, but so far no bites," she concluded. "I don't think anything is going to turn up in Boston."

"How are you holding up emotionally?"

Leave it to Clare to get right to the heart of the problem. "I've been better," Morgan admitted. "The thing is, my work was my life, you know? Since I was let go, I feel…I don't know. Useless, maybe. Like my life isn't worth anything. I'm not even sure who I am anymore."

"Oh, Morgan, you are so much more than your job! You always have been. And your worth doesn't depend on a paycheck. God doesn't value us based on what job we have, or how much we earn, or how high we've risen on the corporate ladder. He doesn't judge us by what we accomplish in a worldly sense, but by who we are and the people whose lives have been made better because of us."

Morgan conceded that Clare might be right. The trouble was, she didn't fare too well on that score, either. Most of her adult life had been devoted to getting ahead. In general, the things she did for other people had a hidden agenda. Even her work on the Good Shepherd board had been dictated by Aunt Jo, and Morgan was only complying so she could get her inheritance. Unlike Grant, she had no altruistic motives. His debt to the camp had been paid long ago, but he still gave of himself unselfishly to help others. She felt small in comparison, which only depressed her further.

"Listen, Morgan, I have a thought," Clare said as the silence lengthened. "Why don't you spend some time at Aunt Jo's cottage? You need to put in four weeks there, anyway. And I'm sure you can conduct your job search just as easily from there, with the Internet and all. Besides, you owe it to yourself to take some time to decompress and unwind after the high-pressure life you've lived all these years."

Morgan considered the suggestion. "That's not a bad idea."

"Think about it, at least," Clare encouraged. Then she grew wistful. "You know, at times like these, I wish we all lived closer together. At least I could give you a hug if I was there. Is there anything I can do long-distance?"

"You could pray," Morgan said, only half teasing.

"You know I'll do that," Clare replied, her voice serious. "And try to trust God on this. I feel that somehow this is part of His plan for you. It may look bad right now, but I have a sense that things will turn out for the best. And call me anytime, okay?"

"Okay. And thanks, Clare."

"I didn't do much."

"You listened. And you cared. That means a lot right now."

"I always care, Morgan. Go to Maine. Trust in God. And I'll keep praying."

As Morgan hung up, she felt better somehow. Connecting with Clare had restored some semblance of normalcy to her life, if only briefly. And her sister's advice had been good. At least some of it. It did make sense to go to Maine. The God part, she was less sure about. It had been a long time since she'd trusted in anyone but herself. But even if her own faith was shaky—at best—she was glad Clare still had a solid relationship with the Lord.

Because she could use all the prayers she could get.

"Grant? It's Morgan. I wanted to let you know that I put a first draft of the Good Shepherd fund-raising campaign plan in the mail to you today."

Grant punched some numbers into the microwave, then shifted the phone to his other ear and sat in a wooden chair at his tiny kitchen table to wait for his dinner to get warm. "Great. Thanks. I'll distribute them to the rest of the board before the next meeting."

"Sounds good. If anyone has any comments before then, let me know."

"Okay."

Grant expected her to conduct the call in her typical style—dispense with chit-chat, get right down to business, then hang up. But that didn't seem to be her inclination today. He sensed that something was on her mind, and thought back to the board meeting two weeks before, when she'd been so distressed. He'd tried without success that day to give her an opening to share her problem. And he'd tried with even less success since then to push thoughts of her aside. Maybe she would be more receptive to an overture today.

"Is there something else we need to discuss?" he asked when the silence lengthened.

"Actually, I was planning to come back to Maine and spend some time at the cottage," she told him.

"Okay. I'll make sure everything's ready for you. When did you want to come up?"

"In a week or so. Maybe ten days. I can let you know for sure when it gets a little closer."

"How long will you be staying this time?"

There was a slight pause. "Indefinitely."

Morgan's voice was a bit unsteady, and there was a quality in it that Grant had never heard before. She sounded…uncertain. Maybe even embarrassed. As if her confidence had been dealt a powerful blow. And it didn't take a genius to figure out why. Based on what she'd told him about her dilemma of trying to juggle the demands of her career with the stipulations in Jo's will, he could only conclude that her sudden ability to spend time in Maine meant that something had happened with her job. Something bad. At least in Morgan's mind.

He knew he was treading on shaky ground, but even though she might rebuff his questions again, he felt compelled to ask. He sensed that she was hurting and was in need of a sympathetic ear.

"So you've managed to work something out with the job?" he asked, choosing his words with care.

When she hesitated, he expected her to brush him aside. But she surprised him by answering.

"The job isn't an issue anymore. My firm was taken over by another company, and a number of people were laid off. I was one of the casualties. But I'm working on lining something else up."

Grant heard the bravado in her voice and recognized it for exactly what it was—a veneer. And a thin one, at that. Knowing her work ethic and her priorities, he could only imagine what a devastating blow her job loss had been to her identity, her ego, her very sense of self. And even if he disagreed with her work-comes-first attitude, he still felt sorry for her. It was clear that her whole world had been turned upside down. And that was something he could definitely relate to.

"I'm sorry, Morgan," he said softly.

"These things happen. But I'll survive. And looking on the bright side, it makes meeting Aunt Jo's residency stipulation a breeze." She tried for a light tone, but her voice was laced with pain.

Grant knew she was deeply upset. But he admired her spunk. She might be hurting on the inside, but she was doing her best to keep up a brave front to the world. What the emotional cost was, he wasn't sure.

"Well, until something else turns up, why

don't you look on this as a vacation? Jo always found her time in Maine to be very relaxing. Maybe this will give you a chance to decompress a little."

"You sound like my sister," Morgan replied. "She said almost the same thing when I spoke with her."

"I have a feeling I'd like your sister."

"Yeah. I have a feeling you would, too." In fact, both her sisters—A.J. and Clare—seemed far more on Grant's wavelength than she did. Especially freespirited A.J., who was saddled with a buttoned-up business partner who sounded more like Morgan's cup of tea.

And as she ended the call, Morgan wondered yet again.

What had Aunt Jo been thinking?

Chapter Seven

⤸

Thank heaven the weather was better on this drive north, Morgan thought as she pulled onto Seaside's main street. Though the ground was snow-covered, the sky was deep blue, the sunshine glorious. And she hadn't gotten lost once, she congratulated herself, as she rolled to a stop in front of the town's sole grocery store. This time she was going to stock up on provisions *before* she went to the cottage. She'd learned her lesson the last time, when she'd almost ended up with soup and tuna for Christmas dinner.

Shopping in the small store took far less time than she expected. Probably because there was such a small selection. Marshall's General Store couldn't hold a candle to the megastores in Boston in terms of merchandise. But when Morgan noticed the pot-bellied stove in one corner, where two patrons were playing checkers, she had to admit that what the store lacked in variety, it made up for in atmosphere.

Dusk was beginning to descend as she started down the secondary road to the cottage, and she again noticed a distinct contrast to Boston. Rush hour there would be in full swing. Here, cars were few and far between. After the last hectic week, when she'd been scrambling to put her trendy, minimalist furnishings into storage, close up her apartment and tie up other loose ends, she welcomed the quiet.

The past few days had also been emotionally trying, because as she'd wrapped up her life in Boston, she'd had an overwhelming sense that she would never call the city home again. That had left her feeling even more uncertain about the future. And for a woman who had always had everything carefully planned, it was not a comfortable place to be.

Morgan tried to put those depressing thoughts aside as she pulled to a stop in front of the cottage and began to unload her belongings. She'd brought only the clothes she thought she might need for the next month, as well as her printer/fax and laptop, so it didn't take long to settle in. And she'd bought enough groceries to last several days, so she didn't have to venture out if she didn't want to. And she didn't particularly want to.

By the time she'd unpacked her clothes and set up her computer, she realized she was starving. She selected a microwave dinner, then flipped on the TV to catch the end of the news while she waited for her meal to heat. Nothing much caught her attention until the last story, a feature on Valentine's Day.

With a start, she realized it was February 14. In years past, her life had been so busy, her job so demanding, that holidays had just been a minor blip on her radar. If she'd thought about Valentine's Day at all, it had only been as a vague reminder that one of these days she needed to pencil romance into her calendar. A husband and family were certainly on her agenda. Someday. But she'd never quite gotten around to them. There had been other, more pressing priorities.

Priorities that had robbed her of something precious—and priceless.

That realization had come to her at Christine's funeral, but it had been hammered home when she'd found herself jobless and been forced to acknowledge that she'd spent her whole life chasing a dream that had no real substance, that couldn't sustain her in the most important ways.

If she hadn't lost her job, she might have reached the pinnacle of success someday. Perhaps she'd have been powerful and wealthy and respected in the business world. But she had a feeling she would also have been alone, that she would never have found the time for the things that gave life its real meaning, the things that mattered in the end.

Even more disheartening was the fact that it might already be too late to find those things. At thirty-five, she wasn't exactly over the hill. But the tick of her biological clock was starting to get pretty loud. And eligible men weren't exactly coming out of the woodwork. Maybe she'd already lost her chance for love, she admitted with a sinking feeling in the pit of her stomach.

And that was a totally depressing thought for Valentine's Day.

The knock on the cottage door startled Morgan, and she jerked, dropping the log she'd just retrieved from the deck. In the past couple of days she'd become accustomed to the quiet of Serenity Point, which was broken only by the sound of the sea lapping against Aunt Jo's tiny beach and the raucous calls of the gulls. So the sharp rapping jangled her nerves.

She glanced down at the floor, now littered with bits of bark, then headed toward the door. It was too dark to see out the window, so she cracked the door open just enough to peek out. When she saw Grant on the other side, she shut the door and slid the chain back, then pulled the door wide.

"Come in. I'm still being cautious, as you can see."

He moved past her, bringing with him a puff of cold and the bracing scent of spruce.

"We don't have much crime around here," he reassured her as he pulled off his gloves. "But it never hurts to be careful. Sorry for the impromptu visit, but I just wanted to make sure everything was okay. I meant to stop by sooner, but it's been busy at the shop."

"Everything's fine. The electricity and phones are working, and I have a fully stocked kitchen this time, thanks to a stop at the quaint general store—which seems to double as a social club."

He flashed her a brief grin. "You must have seen Ralph and Joe playing checkers in the back."

"How did you know?"

"They're fixtures at the place." He glanced toward the living room. "I see you're making use of the fireplace."

"That's one luxury I didn't have in Boston. Thank you for putting the wood on the deck. Can I offer you some coffee?"

"That sounds good. Thanks. How's the job search going?"

"Nothing yet. But I'm working on it."

"I'm sure something will turn up. You obviously have talent, based on the plan you created for Good Shepherd. I've passed it on to the rest of the board, and so far I've gotten a great response. Everyone is excited about the possibilities and anxious to get everything finalized at the next meeting."

"Good. I should have some additional information by then. I'm still working my contacts. Go ahead and have a seat in the living room."

Grant strolled into the room and bent to pick up the log Morgan had dropped. As he crouched to place it in the fireplace, he angled his body so that he could observe her without her notice. Her movements were awkward, as if she was stressed out and had way more nervous energy than she knew what to do with. She seemed somehow fragile—almost brittle—as if she might break at the slightest provocation. And when she joined him and held out the coffee, her hand was trembling. With a self-conscious blush, she reached out to steady it with her other hand.

As Grant took the mug, their fingers brushed. Hers were cold, and for the briefest instant he felt an urge to take her hands in his, cocoon her slender fingers, let the warmth of his skin seep into hers. It was an unexpected, disconcerting—and totally inappropriate—impulse, and he took a startled, abrupt step back.

Morgan gave him a surprised look, and he felt his neck grow warm. Sorry now that he'd agreed to stay for coffee, he figured the best plan was to finish it off as fast as possible and get out. He took a long sip—and almost scalded his throat. When he started to cough, Morgan moved closer and placed a hand on his arm.

"Are you okay?" she asked in concern.

As a matter of fact, he wasn't. He was so close to her, he could see tiny gold flecks in her deep green eyes. And the faint sprinkling of freckles that dotted her silky, fair skin. She also had long, sweeping eyelashes, he noted. And her soft, full lips were…

Grant's mouth went dry, and he drew in a sharp breath. This was all wrong. He didn't even like Morgan Williams. Yet he was acting as if he was attracted to her. Then another deeply disturbing emotion joined the jumble of feelings he was already experiencing.

Guilt.

What on earth was wrong with him? He'd just lost his wife, whom he'd loved with all his heart. He shouldn't be attracted to this woman—or any woman. He needed to leave. Now. Yet he couldn't seem to get his feet to co-operate.

Morgan stared back at Grant, unable to interpret the look in his eyes. But she was very aware of their intense blueness. As well as the fine lines that radiated from their corners, which told her that at one time he had laughed more than he did now. There were other lines in his face, too. Lines of weariness and strain. But also appealing lines that spoke of character and maturity. She let her gaze trace the strong angle of his jaw, which held just a hint of five-o'clock shadow, then wander to his neatly trimmed hair, noting the fine sprinkling of silver among the sandy-brown strands. Finally, she looked again into his eyes. They were still focused on her, and for just a moment, before he shuttered them, she thought she detected a glimmer of…attraction? But that was absurd. They had been thrown together by circumstance, not choice. And they had very little in common. She didn't think he even liked her. And he had just lost the woman he loved.

Yet there was something between them.

Something she'd never before experienced and had no idea how to describe. She'd always known Grant was a handsome man, with an appealing combination of strength and sensitivity. But she'd never been attracted to him before, probably because she hadn't let herself be. They were too different, after all, and she'd had other priorities. Yet right now their differences seemed less important, and her priorities were beginning to shift. Which opened up a lot of possibilities—none of which she was ready to consider. Especially in light of her currently chaotic life.

The sudden ringing of the phone broke the spell, and Grant looked as relieved as Morgan felt when she excused herself to answer it. Even though it was just someone soliciting a donation, she took her time with the call, giving herself a chance to regain her balance. By the time she returned, Grant had finished his coffee and pulled on his gloves. This time she made it a point to keep a good distance between them.

"I need to run," he said.

"Thanks for stopping by."

"Let me know if you need anything."

"I will."

As their stilted conversation came to an end, he made a beeline for the door. She followed, and he turned to her before stepping outside. "I hope things go well with the job search."

"Thanks. Me, too. I'm not used to having so much time on my hands." She summoned up a smile. "But at least this gives me more time to work on the Good Shepherd project."

"Well, that's our gain, though I'm sorry it's at your expense."

"It's helping me keep my skills honed," she replied with a shrug. "And in touch with real people. It gets pretty quiet out here."

In the fast-paced world of business Morgan was used to, she must have interacted with dozens of people every day, he realized, his resolve to make a rapid escape faltering. Living in a remote cottage in Maine had to be an abrupt change for her. Isolation could be good in some ways, allowing quiet time for reflection, but based on her comment, he suddenly had a feeling she might be getting too much of it. The dark shadows under her eyes indicated sleeplessness, the tremor in her hands implied taut nerves and the weight loss suggested that her appetite wasn't good. He knew firsthand those were all signs of depression. While Morgan struck him as a strong woman, even strong people could cave, given sufficient stress. And there was no question that having your world turned upside down fell into that category.

Grant didn't think Morgan was the type to take any sort of desperate measures, but he didn't know her that well. And contact with other people couldn't hurt. Except she didn't know anyone up here. Other than him and his family. After the unsettling episode by the fireplace, Grant didn't think it would be wise for him to spend too much time with her alone. But maybe he could call on Kit for help. She had a lot of empathy and was good at dealing with people. And they had seemed to hit it off at Christmas.

"Jo chose this spot years ago because she wanted a place that felt removed from the world," Grant responded.

Morgan smiled. "I'd say she found it."

"Have you explored the property at all?" Exercise wasn't a bad idea, either, he decided.

"No. I wasn't sure where the boundaries were, and there's been so much snow."

"She owned three acres, so this whole little spit of land was hers. There's a bench down at the very point that looks out to sea. It was one of her favorite places. The roads are clear now, too, and lightly traveled, if you're in the mood for a walk."

"I'll keep that in mind."

"Take care, then."

When Grant reached his truck, he looked back toward the cottage. Morgan's lithe form was silhouetted in the doorway, warm light spilling around her. She raised a hand in farewell, and he responded before climbing behind the wheel. As he put the truck in gear and drove into the darkness, he glanced in the rearview mirror. She was still standing there, looking lovely. And appealing.

Grant forced himself to focus on the road. For almost three long years he'd been alone, caught in a time warp, as days turned into weeks, and weeks turned into years, while Christine clung tenuously to life. And each day, as he'd sat by her bedside and held her unresponsive hand, he'd ached for the simple pleasures of the happy marriage he had once known. The tender touches. The warm, intimate smiles. The private jokes. The cuddles by the fire on cold winter evenings. The sense of contentment, and the feeling that all was right with the world.

Perhaps that basic human need for connection explained his reaction to Morgan tonight. Perhaps it wasn't so much her, as the fact that the emptiness of his solitary existence had finally caught up with him. Perhaps she had simply been in the right place at the right time, and he would have reacted the same way to any woman.

But somehow he had a feeling that his explanation was far too simple.

And not likely to stand the test of time.

It had been one of her most depressing days so far. Three rejections, all from firms that she'd had high hopes about.

No one wanted her.

For the first time since losing her job, Morgan felt tears well up in her eyes, and the bitter taste of despair was on her tongue. Suddenly the walls of Aunt Jo's cottage seemed to close in on her, and in desperation she grabbed her purse and headed out to her car. She needed a change of scene.

For a long time, Morgan drove aimlessly, unaware of her surroundings until she found herself pulling up in front of the small, white church where she'd attended Christmas services. She had no recollection of heading toward Seaside, had made no conscious decision to stop at the church. But as she stared up at the tall white spire pointing heavenward, it felt right to be here. Maybe, in this place that had brought back so many memories of comfort and peace from her childhood, she might find the consolation she yearned for.

Of course, chances were slim that the door would be unlocked on a weekday. But it was worth checking out, as long as she was here. She needed help, and had no idea where else to turn.

Much to Morgan's surprise, the door opened when she gave it a push. She stepped into the empty church and stood in the back, letting the peace and stillness steal over her. The tall, clear windows that reached all the way to the upper level offered a stunning view of the deep blue wintry sky, and bright light streamed through, spotlighting the simple interior in striking bands. Unfortunately, the heat in the building didn't seem to be turned on, and a shiver ran through her. She shoved her hands in the pockets of her coat, sorry now that she'd left her gloves in the car. But it wasn't worth making a trip back outside to retrieve them. She didn't plan to stay long.

Morgan moved to the last pew and sank down. For the past few weeks she'd been searching for answers to questions about why her life had been turned upside down, and deeper questions, about the very meaning of her existence. She'd spent thirteen years building a career in advertising to the exclusion of everything else—she'd neglected her sisters, given up any semblance of a personal life and turned away from God. And what did she have to show for her sacrifices?

Nothing.

Morgan's shoulders drooped and she lowered her head, fighting back tears. The things she'd given up were the very things that could sustain her now, if she'd nurtured them. She could count on A.J. and Clare, of course, despite her negligence. They'd always been there for each other. But they didn't understand why she'd become so obsessed with success. And she was beginning to wonder why, herself. True, she'd never wanted to end up like her mother, struggling just to make ends meet because of the untimely death of her husband. But she'd taken the quest for security to an extreme, only to fail in the end, anyway.

She'd already rehashed her personal life on Valentine's Day. She was well aware that the husband and family she'd always put at the bottom of her list might well be unattainable now.

And as for falling away from God…perhaps that had been her biggest mistake. She couldn't blame her background for that misstep. She'd grown up in a church-going, God-centered household, and A.J. and Clare had managed to hang on to their faith through far tougher times than she'd ever encountered. So had Grant. Why had she let it go? Was it because she was *too* successful? Had she come to believe that she didn't need God anymore?

Morgan suspected that that was exactly what had happened. Maybe it was easier to hold on to your faith when times were tough, when you needed an anchor and a guiding hand. Success, on the other hand, could give you a false sense of independence and self-reliance, even arrogance, making it easier to push God aside and think you didn't need Him.

But she needed Him now.

It had been a long time since Morgan had prayed. So long that she'd almost forgotten how. And she felt awkward about initiating a conversation with the God she'd long ago relegated to, at best, a secondary role in her life. But she had nowhere else to turn for help. So she knew she had to try.

Lord, I'm afraid You might have forgotten who I am, she began, her words silent and halting. *But Clare and A.J. would tell me that isn't true, that You are with us always, even when we abandon You. I hope they're right. Because I haven't been Your most faithful servant. I've made a lot of mistakes, maybe the biggest one being that I didn't think I needed You anymore. That I could handle life on my own. But I don't think that now, Lord. My life is a mess, and I don't know where to go from here. I don't even know who I am anymore. I've gotten so caught up in the quest for worldly success that I've lost touch with the things that really matter, the things that truly count.*

I'd like to get back on track, Lord. But I need guid-ance. Please help me find my way home again. Show me the path that You want me to follow. Right now I feel like I'm lost, wandering in a desert with no star to guide me. I know I don't deserve Your help after all of the wrong turns I've made, but I'll try to put my trust in Your mercy and forgiveness and hope that You'll take pity on your wayward daughter.

I also ask, Lord, that You look with special favor on Grant, who has been so kind to me and who is struggling to deal with the loss of the woman he loved. And please be with Clare and A.J., whose loyal love and support has always been such a blessing to me, even though I've often taken it for granted. Amen.

Morgan felt a tear slip from her eye. Then another. She didn't try to stop them. That would be futile. Because she needed to cry.

For all the mistakes she'd made.

For all the things she'd missed.

For all the wrong choices she'd made.

And for the yesterdays she couldn't change that could very well affect all of her tomorrows.

Grant gave the screwdriver one final twist, then tested the door of the church's vestment cabinet, noting with satisfaction that it now moved with ease on its hinges. He put the tool back in his kit, closed and fastened the lid and checked his watch. He still needed to go back to the shop and help his father and Uncle Pete load the dining-room set they planned to deliver tomorrow.

Grant flipped off the light in the vesting room, then stepped out into the sanctuary, his rubber-soled work shoes noiseless on the marble floor. He started toward the back door, but came to an abrupt stop when he noticed the solitary figure in the back pew. Though her head was bowed, he had no trouble recognizing Morgan's distinctive, dark copper hair.

Grant hesitated, uncertain how to proceed. With her slumped posture and bowed head, she was the picture of dejection, and his heart ached for her. She looked so alone, so in need of a friend. She must be feeling really low if she'd turned to God for help, given her comment at Christmas about church attendance being a rare occurrence.

He considered calling out to her, then thought better of it. Knowing how hard she was trying to keep up a good public front, he was sure she'd be embarrassed to be caught in this very private, personal moment.

Grant glanced again at his watch. He needed to lock up before he left, and he couldn't do that with Morgan inside. So there was only one course of action. He retreated to the vesting room, then made enough noise to clue her in to his presence.

When he returned to the sanctuary, Morgan was sitting up and looked far more composed— though she seemed a bit startled to discover that he had been the source of the noise. She rose as he moved down the aisle, and despite the smile she summoned up, he saw the lingering sadness in the depths of her eyes. As well as clear evidence of recent tears, which she'd tried without complete success to erase.

"Hi. I didn't expect to find you here," he greeted her.

She gave him a rueful smile. "Me, neither. I just started driving, and the next thing I knew

I found myself pulling up in front of the church. I was surprised to find the door open."

"I stopped by to fix a hinge on a vestment cabinet I made for the church several years ago. I'm sorry if I disturbed you."

"I was just talking to God. Or trying to," she amended.

"He's a good listener."

"It's a pretty one-sided conversation, though."

"You do have to listen in a different way to hear His voice," Grant acknowledged, smiling.

"I guess I'll have to relearn that skill, then, because I could use some good advice."

"About the job situation?"

"About life in general. Things are kind of…a mess right now."

Her voice broke, and much to Morgan's horror, a tear slipped from her eye and trailed down her cheek. Embarrassed, she reached up to brush it away. "Sorry. I don't usually lose control like this."

"You've had a lot thrown at you these past few weeks," Grant commiserated, realizing anew the fragility of Morgan's emotional state. He had concluded a long time ago that she was a woman who tended to keep her emotions on a tight leash. The fact that her control had slipped meant she was teetering right on the edge. It was clear that frightened her. And, to his surprise, him as well.

"But I should be able to cope better than this," she said, cutting herself no slack. "A job loss isn't the end of the world, after all."

"It's the end of the world you knew before." He gestured to the pew. "Would you like to sit and talk for a few minutes?"

Morgan was about to say no, but when she looked into his eyes, she saw an empathy born of pain and disappointment that tempted her to confide in him, to share her feelings, to take advantage of the sympathetic ear he was offering. And she also sensed that she could trust this man with the secrets of her heart, that he would never betray her confidence.

Morgan needed to talk with someone. She'd opened her heart to God, but as Grant had told her, she had to learn to listen for His voice in a different way—a skill she hadn't yet mastered. In the meantime, a flesh-and-blood person was willing to talk with her, to offer his support and understanding, to give her feedback she could hear right away.

She drew a deep breath and made her decision—but she gave him an out in case he was having second thoughts about his offer. "Are you sure you have time?"

Grant nodded. As if to emphasize his point, he sat down. "I'm in no hurry."

Morgan joined him. "I feel guilty burdening you with my problems when you have your own to deal with. Mine seem so petty in comparison. When I think of all the years you were faithful to Christine, only to lose her in the end…I can't even begin to fathom that kind of heartbreak."

Grant looked away, drawing in a deep breath to ease the pain that gripped his heart. He waited until it had ebbed to a dull throb before turning back to her. "We all have our crosses to bear, Morgan. I've had a long time to learn how to live with mine—with God's help. Yours is new. And from what you've said, I don't think you have quite the foundation of faith to fall back on that I have. So don't feel guilty. I'm glad to offer a friendly ear. Sometimes a different perspective can offer new insights." He angled his body toward her, his eyes warm and sympathetic. "You haven't said much about the situation other than the bare facts, but I sense that this has been a devastating experience for you," he ventured.

She nodded and looked down at her clasped hands. She'd been so self-reliant for so long, so in control, that it was hard to let go, to admit that she didn't have all the answers. Which was due to pride, of course. She didn't want to lose face. Yet she felt safe with this man, somehow knowing deep in her heart that he would treat her confidences with gentleness and respect. And that gave her the courage to put her pride aside and admit that maybe she wasn't quite the superwoman she'd always thought she was.

So, in a halting voice, Morgan told him of her job loss, her sense of betrayal, and her feelings of failure, isolation and diminished self-worth.

"I know in my heart that I'm more than my job," she concluded. "And just in case I'd forgotten, my sister, Clare, was quick to remind me of that. But so much of my life has been focused on my work that the rest of me has somehow gotten lost. And I'm just not sure how to find it again. Or even where to look."

Grant had been listening with quiet attentiveness, but now he leaned forward, his eyes intent. "It's there, Morgan. But it may be buried pretty far down after all these years. Maybe you just need to give yourself some time."

"Patience has never been my strong suit," she admitted.

"A lot of us struggle with that."

She gave him an appraising look. "You strike me as a very patient man."

He shook his head. "It doesn't come to me naturally. But I learned a lot these past few years. About acknowledging that we aren't always in charge. About letting go. About trusting that things happen in God's time, not always in ours."

"Those are hard lessons. Especially when being in charge, taking control, and getting ahead as fast as possible are the values of the world you've lived in."

"Not every world is like that."

"Yours certainly doesn't seem to be," she conceded "Have you always lived here?"

"Maine is home. I always knew it was where I belonged."

"But didn't you ever aspire to more?"

He looked at her steadily. "I have my faith, and my family and work I love. What more is there?"

Morgan didn't know how to respond. Perhaps because there was no answer. He'd pretty much summed up everything that counted. Of all the successful men she'd ever met in the business world, many of them famous and powerful, none had radiated the quiet confidence that Grant did. He seemed like a man who had found his place in the world and was content with it. There was no restlessness, no grasping, no struggle to meet some nebulous definition of worldly success. And despite the tragedy that had changed his life forever, he still seemed like a man at peace with himself. She envied him that.

A sudden shiver ran through her, and she pulled her coat more tightly around her body. She hadn't intended to stay long enough in the chilly church for the cold to seep through the thin, wool fabric. It was time to go.

But she didn't want to. Here, in this man's presence, she felt a sense calm, of caring that was a balm to her soul, and she didn't want the moment to end. Because she knew that once she left this place, and this man, she would again be assailed by doubts. So she rubbed her hands together for warmth, hoping to prolong the interlude.

Grant's gaze dropped to her hands. He hadn't missed her shiver, either. Morgan's fashionable wool coat might be fine for running between buildings in Boston, but it wasn't designed for extended exposure to the cold. And the church was very cold. She must be chilled to the bone.

Without even stopping to think, Grant reached for her hands and clasped her icy fingers in his warm ones. "You're cold," he murmured. "Does this help?"

She went perfectly still, her attention riveted on their entwined hands. Hers had been swallowed by his lean, strong fingers, which held them in a gentle, sure grasp. She *had* been cold. But now she was warm. Grant's touch sent a jolt surging through her, causing a flush to rise on her cheeks. She knew his gesture was a simple act of kindness, motivated by a concern for her well-being. Nothing more. Yet she felt far more. Safe. Protected. Cared for.

And attracted to this man—way more than was prudent.

No one had ever evoked that exact combination of feelings in her. And she was confused by her reaction. She only knew one thing with certainty. She needed to get herself under control. Fast.

As Grant stared down at Morgan's bowed head, he realized that touching her had been a mistake. It felt good. Too good. Which meant it was wrong. Somehow, his innocent gesture had gone awry. He should never have taken her hands in his. There had been a simpler way to warm her up—escort her to her car, where she could turn on the heater.

He was just about to release her when she looked up at him, and the longing he saw in her eyes made his heart stop, then race on. His mouth went dry, and he suddenly he wanted to do more than just hold her hands.

Grant had no idea how to deal with the yearning or the unexpected impulses that swept over him. All he knew was that acting on them would be wrong. It was way too soon after Christine's death to have these kinds of feelings. Yet there they were. Along with soul-searing, crushing guilt.

He dropped Morgan's hands and stood, jamming his own hands in his pockets. "It's too cold in here," he said, his voice as uneven as rough-hewn wood. "You'll be better off in your car, with the heater cranked up."

Morgan stood as well, her own eyes now distressed and confused. Like Grant, she stuck her hands in her pockets. "You're probably right." Her voice was as shaky as his.

In silence, she followed him to the door and stepped outside, waiting as he locked it behind them. Then she turned to him with a forced smile. "Thanks for listening."

"Sure. Anytime."

But even as he said the words, Grant resolved that there wouldn't be another time.

There couldn't be.
Because Morgan was too lovely.
And he was too lonely.

Chapter Eight

"Yoo-hoo! Anybody home?"

Morgan walked to the edge of Aunt Jo's cottage and peered around the side. An SUV she didn't recognize was parked in front. "I'm around back," she called.

A moment later Kit appeared. "Hi there! In the mood for a visitor?"

"Absolutely. I've gotten kind of tired of talking to the squirrels and chipmunks."

Chuckling, Kit joined her on the deck. "Sounds like a case of cabin fever to me. Are you going stir-crazy?"

"Not really. I've been spending a lot of time on my job search and working on the Good Shepherd project. So I keep busy. And I've started taking long walks. At your brother's suggestion."

"He comes up with a good idea now and then," Kit said with a smile, turning to admire the vista of the sea. "I always thought Serenity Point had the best view in the area. But it's a little chilly for deck-sitting today, isn't it?"

"I just came out for a breath of fresh air. Would you like some coffee?"

"Sure. And I brought a crumb cake from the bakery. They have the world's best," she said, holding up a small, white box.

"Mmm. That sounds tempting." Morgan led the way inside. "Just move that stuff on the table aside while I get the coffee. I was working on the camp project right before you came, and it sort of took over."

"How's it going?"

"Not bad. I think the board will be pleased with some of the things I've lined up. Are you involved at all with the camp?"

"Only in a minor way. I don't know if Grant told you, but I'm a graphic designer. I work out of my home, and I do most of the design and layouts for any printed materials the camp needs."

Morgan set two mugs of coffee, plates and forks, on the table, then handed Kit a knife. "You can do the honors. And no, Grant didn't tell me that. I figured being the mother of fifteen-year-old twins, as well as a preacher's wife, would keep you busy enough."

Kit laughed as she cut them each a generous piece of cake. "Those two roles are pretty demanding," she agreed. "But I love graphic design, too, so I've always managed to keep my hand in the field. Working for myself, out of my house, gives me a lot of flexibility and control. I can take as much or as little work as I want."

"It sounds like you have an ideal arrangement." Morgan propped her chin in her hand, her expression wistful. "A career you enjoy, but time for other things, as well."

"That's true. I can't imagine not working at all, but I never wanted that to be my only focus."

"I guess I never learned that lesson. At least, not until recently. And then not by choice."

"Grant told me your firm was acquired and that you lost your job in the reorganization. I'm sorry, Morgan. That had to be tough."

"I had quite a pity party for a while," she admitted, striving for a light tone. "But I don't miss the stress or the pressure. I do miss the work, though."

"Have you thought about freelancing? Or starting your own small agency?"

Morgan looked at her in surprise. "It's pretty

tough to compete with the big guys. They've got the market sewn up in Boston."

"So you're committed to staying there?"

"No. In fact, I've expanded my job search. I haven't had any responses yet, though."

"I'm sure it just takes time to connect."

"Well, patience isn't my strong suit, as I told Grant a few days ago. I just want things to be settled. Frankly, I wish I could find the kind of contentment that he appears to have. Despite the terrible tragedy with Christine, he seems like a man who's found his place in the world and is at peace."

"That's true. He's completely happy with his life here, and he gets great satisfaction from his work. Even though he went away to college to please Dad, I think Grant always knew he'd come home."

"He went to college?" Morgan said in surprise.

"Yes. In Boston. He has a degree in electrical engineering. Finished top in his class and had more job offers than he could keep track of. But it wasn't what he wanted. And deep in his heart, I think Dad was glad when Grant came home, because the cabinet shop has been in the family for three generations. But he wanted to make sure Grant at least had other options and something to fall back on."

"I had no idea about Grant's educational background."

"Dad and Mom wanted both of us to go to college. That may have been the one thing they agreed on."

Kit's comment piqued Morgan's curiosity, but she didn't want Grant's sister to think she was prying. "I saw your mother at the funeral," she ventured.

"I was glad she came. She lives in Boston, and doesn't always make it up for family events. She's vice president of a major financial institution."

When Kit mentioned the name, Morgan's eyebrows rose. "Wow! I'm impressed."

"It's what she always wanted. She went back to school right after I was born and got her degree in economics. Then she went on for her MBA through a weekend program in Boston. She worked in Brunswick for a while, but when I was fifteen and Grant was eleven, she was offered a job in Boston at the firm she's still with. Mom and Dad had been drifting further and further apart by then, anyway. Work had begun to consume more and more of Mom's time, and Dad had taken on most of the household and child-rearing duties. So they parted more or less amicably, and Dad took custody of us."

"So, they're divorced?"

"No. Dad didn't believe in it, and Mom didn't see any reason to push for it. I don't think she had any interest in getting married again, anyway," Kit said, her tone matter-of-fact. "She had great ambitions, and another marriage would have been too much of a distraction from her work."

Kit seemed at ease with the subject, so Morgan felt comfortable asking a few more questions. "Does your Mom stay in touch?"

"Most of the time she sends a card on our birthdays and holidays, and she tries to come up for important family functions. Like Christine's funeral. But our contact is infrequent, at best."

"You seem okay with that," Morgan commented.

"I am now. But it was hard at first. Even though she was busy with work when she lived in Seaside, at least she was physically present some of the time. I missed that when she left. And like Grant, I was angry. I just manifested it in a different way, by withdrawing more into myself. But over time I realized that Mom should never have gotten married and had kids. Some people just aren't cut out for that. And Dad was great. He was a rock through the whole thing. It was a lot tougher on Grant, who was still a little kid when she left. He had some rough times."

"He mentioned that he got into trouble at school, and that Aunt Jo took a special interest in him. In fact, he said she was the one who discovered Good Shepherd."

"That's true. Jo was a godsend for Grant. We all loved her, but she took him under her wing. And even though she was only here a few weeks a year, she made it a point to stay in touch often. Which is something Mom never did. And Grant never forgot that."

"It sounds like there are still some bad feelings," Morgan reflected.

"There are. I think Grant's forgiven Mom, and even understands that she never meant to hurt us. That she just wasn't cut out for the role. But Grant is a man who honors his commitments. And he's never forgotten that she didn't honor hers. So I don't think he respects her very much. And he certainly doesn't feel anything for her, or have any emotional ties."

"I can understand how he feels. And I admire you for being able to get past that."

"It doesn't do any good to think about what might have been. This was obviously God's plan for our family. And we've been blessed in so many other ways. I have Bill and the girls, and Dad and Uncle Pete are great. Grant's had the roughest time all around. Sometimes I don't know how he found the strength to go on. I'm not sure I could have done it in his place." She drew a deep breath, then forced herself to smile. "Enough of that depressing stuff. I had an idea I wanted to pass on. You don't sound like you're interested in going freelance right now on a permanent basis, but would you consider taking some small, short-term jobs while you're waiting to connect somewhere?"

"I suppose so. But I don't know where they'd come from."

"Well, I do work for some agencies who have clients all over this area. They're smaller businesses that can't afford big-agency fees, but they still need help with advertising and marketing. Can I drop your name a few places?"

"Why not? I could use the income."

"Great." Kit glanced at her watch, took a last swallow of coffee, then stood. "I've bent your ear long enough for one day. Grant always says I can outtalk any politician, so I hope I didn't overwhelm you."

"Hardly. It was nice to have some company. And the coffee cake was great."

"We'll do it again soon," Kit promised with a grin.

After waving Grant's sister off, Morgan closed the door and returned to the kitchen to refill her coffee cup. And as she cut herself a second slice of the decadent coffee cake, her heart felt lighter than it had in weeks. Kit's upbeat attitude had certainly been therapeutic. And she also felt she had a better handle on what made Grant tick—as well as a better understanding of why there'd been such tension between the two of them in the beginning. With her single-minded focus on work, she'd reminded him of his mother. But she'd learned a lot since then. And her focus was changing, which should smooth out their relationship a bit.

Not that it mattered, of course. Grant and she were never destined to be more than friends. His love for his wife was still strong and true. And Morgan didn't plan to take up permanent residence in Aunt Jo's cottage.

But a little niggling voice in the back of her mind reminded her of the spark that had leapt between them, first here in the cottage, then again at church. It was the kind of spark that often led to more than friendship. The question was, could they contain it? Could they tame it so that it fueled friendship but stopped short of romance?

Morgan was willing to try.

But based on Grant's abrupt escape from church, she wasn't so sure he was.

Nor, in all honesty, was she sure they could.

"I think we'd better get started. Could everyone take their seats?"

Grant had delayed the start of the February Good Shepherd board meeting as long as possible, hoping that Morgan would show up, but they were already ten minutes behind schedule and there was still no sign of her. He'd seen her at church on Sunday, and since she'd mentioned the meeting, he knew she hadn't forgotten about it. So where was she?

Grant had toyed with the idea of offering her a ride today. It had seemed silly to take two cars all the way to Portland. But he was still unsettled after their encounter in the empty church. If she'd been in an accident, though, he'd never forgive himself. The roads were slick, and she was still unfamiliar with the narrow byways. Maybe she'd had car trouble. Or...

The door burst open, and as Morgan rushed in, all heads swiveled her direction.

"I'm sorry I'm late," she apologized. "I was

on the phone with something relating to Good Shepherd, and the call took far longer than I expected. But I hope you'll think that the result justifies my tardiness."

"We were just getting started," Grant told her, his unexpected panic at her lateness subsiding as she took a place at the far end of the table. Then he turned back to the group. "I know we're all anxious to discuss the fundraising effort, but let's give Morgan a chance to catch her breath. John, will you lead us in prayer?"

Morgan sent Grant a grateful look before she bowed her head and waited for the gray-haired minister to begin.

"Lord, we ask Your blessing on this work we do in Your name. Please help us discern Your will for us as we embark on our first major fundraising effort. Those of us on the board are Your humble servants, but most of us are not too schooled in these matters. We thank You for sending Morgan to guide our steps so that we can continue to provide this much-needed service to troubled youth. And please watch over all the young people who have passed through the door of Good Shepherd. We ask this in Your name."

After everyone murmured, "Amen," Grant

turned to Morgan. "Do you need a few more minutes?"

"No, I'm set." She opened her briefcase and withdrew some papers. "Before I lay out what I've been working on, though, are there any comments on the preliminary plan I developed?"

"I thought it looked great," Sylvia said. "I'm just anxious to hear the details."

When everyone else nodded their assent, Morgan continued. "Okay. Well, I've been busy since we last met. As some of you know, I spent a number of years with a pretty prominent ad agency in Boston, and during that time I made some good contacts in the corporate world. A lot of the companies I dealt with have excellent charitable outreach efforts, so I called the ones I thought might be interested in assisting with this effort. And I'm happy to tell you, the response was overwhelming."

Morgan ticked down the list of companies that had offered to support the fund-raising dinner/auction, either through direct donations, by buying a table or by offering goods and services.

"So I think the basic cost of the dinner will be covered. Which means that every penny we bring in will go to the camp. But I've saved the best news for last. And that's the call I took right before I drove down here today."

She withdrew a sheet of paper from the stack in front of her. "One of the clients I worked with has a promotional relationship with a prominent singer." When she mentioned the entertainer's name, eyebrows rose around the table. "Anyway, as you know she's been very open about her strong faith and the importance of Christianity in her life. My corporate client offered to speak with her agent to see if she might be willing to entertain at our event, and I spoke with her agent just before I left today. I'm delighted to tell you the answer is yes. She'll waive her usual fee and we'll just need to pick up her expenses, which should be minimal."

A collective gasp went up around the table, and then the room erupted in excited chatter. It took Grant several attempts to restore order, and when quiet finally descended, he turned to Morgan with a smile that warmed her all the way to her toes.

"I think it's safe to say that we're overwhelmed," he said.

A flush rose on her cheeks and her own lips curved in response. "I can't take much credit. My corporate contacts did all the work."

"But you had those contacts. We didn't," Grant pointed out.

"I'm glad I could put them to good use. But there's still a lot to do. I can work on the publicity and promotional materials, but we also need to choose a venue and handle all of the event-planning details."

"The board can take care of that part," Sylvia assured her. "We'll just divide up into committees."

"And I have good news on the alumni list," Mary chimed in. "I've gone through it and identified a number of pretty prominent people in the business and political arena who may be willing to serve on an advisory board and lend their names to our efforts. Grant, as chairman, I thought the invitation should come from you."

"I'll take care of it," he promised. "Just give me the list. Now let's settle on a date for the dinner." After some discussion, the board arrived at both a primary and a back-up date. "Is there anything else we need to do today?"

Everyone turned to Morgan, and she shook her head. "I think everything's under control. Grant, Kit told me that she designs the brochures and print pieces for Good Shepherd. Shall I work with her to put together some layouts for the materials we'll need?"

"Yes. I'll let her know you'll be calling."

Sylvia gave Morgan a thoughtful look. "You know, if you're going to be developing promotional materials, you should visit the camp."

"That's a good idea," Mary concurred. "It's pretty quiet right now, of course. But the facilities are nice, and Joe and Elizabeth would be glad to show you around."

"Grant, why don't you take her out?" Sylvia suggested.

Morgan saw the objection in his eyes even before he voiced it.

"That would take most of a day, Sylvia," he balked.

"Well, with all the time Morgan's put into this effort, I would think that's the least we can do. And you know the place better than all of us put together."

Morgan had no intention of forcing herself on a reluctant guide. "I'm sure I can develop the materials just using the background information that Grant gave me," she stepped in.

"It's not the same," the older woman insisted.

"Sylvia's right," Grant conceded with obvious reluctance, directing his comment to Morgan. "It would be helpful if you took a look." He turned to the older woman. "We'll try to find a time that will work."

The woman gave a satisfied nod. "Good."

A short time later, Grant wrapped up the meeting, and Morgan made a quick escape before he had a chance to stop her, as he had the last time. It was obvious he didn't want to take her to the camp. And while she would like to see it, she didn't intend to put him in an uncomfortable position. If he wanted to contact her about taking a tour, fine. If he didn't, she could still do a credible job on the promotional materials.

Besides, maybe that was safer. She knew Grant had been as shaken as she was after their last meeting. He probably thought it best if they limited their contact.

Intellectually, Morgan knew that that was a smart move.

But it didn't make her heart feel any better.

"Kit, these look great!" Morgan leaned closer to examine the designs for the Good Shepherd materials that the other woman had spread out on the table in Aunt Jo's cottage.

Kit's face flushed with pleasure. "Well, they're very rough. But after we talked on the phone and you faxed over the preliminary copy, I thought I'd go ahead and get a jump on the job given our abbreviated time frame. With the fund-raiser barely two months off, the invitations and brochures need to go out as soon as possible."

"I know. And I appreciate how quickly you tackled this. I don't see any reason to change a thing," Morgan said as she perused the layouts. "I think we should just give them to Grant to share with the board, and then move into production as soon as we have the okay. I should have the copy finalized in the next few days."

"Do you want to run these by him, or shall I?"

Morgan straightened up. "You might as well do it. I'm sort of off the beaten path here, and you see him more often than I do."

Kit gathered the material together and began putting it in her portfolio case. "So when is he going to take you out to the camp?" At Morgan's surprised look, Kit grinned. "I have my sources. I called the office because I needed Mary to e-mail me a JPEG of the logo, and she told me about Sylvia's idea."

"I haven't heard from him yet. And I can put the material together without a visit," Morgan replied, striving for an indifferent tone.

"I'm sure you can. But it would help to see the place. I'll say something to him when I drop these off."

"No!" At Morgan's quick—and vehement—response, Kit turned to her in surprise. Morgan knew she'd overreacted, and made an effort to tone down her reply. "I'm sure he's busy, Kit. It's not necessary."

At Kit's speculative look, Morgan shifted uncomfortably, hoping the other woman wouldn't pursue the subject. She didn't, for which Morgan was grateful.

"Well, whatever. Just e-mail me the final copy. And let me know if the board has any changes. Or I'll let you know, depending on who hears first." She zipped her case and turned to go, then stopped and rummaged in her pocket. "I can't believe I almost left without giving you this." She withdrew a folded slip of paper and held it out. "I talked to Marge Henderson at the Brunswick Tourist Bureau. I do quite a bit of work for them. Anyway, they're looking for someone to design a new marketing program, and I mentioned your name. She said she'd love to hear from you."

Morgan took the slip of paper and smiled. "I guess you weren't kidding about sending me work."

"Hey, there's no obligation. But the opportunity is there if you're interested. Listen, I've got to run. I'll talk to you soon."

"Okay. And thanks."

"My pleasure."

As Morgan closed the door, she glanced again at the slip of paper. It wasn't exactly the big time. But it might be fun.

Besides, it was the only offer she'd had.

"So what gives with you and Morgan?" Kit asked as she pulled the layouts out of her portfolio and handed them to Grant.

"What do you mean?" His tone was cautious, his eyes wary.

"When I asked her if you'd called yet about setting up the camp tour, she said no, then jumped all over me when I told her I'd remind you."

"Maybe she doesn't want to go."

Kit cocked her head, pinned him with her astute eyes, then shook her head. "Sorry. Don't buy it."

"Why not?"

"I think she thinks you don't want to take her."

"You're reading too much into this."

"I don't think so."

Grant expelled an exasperated sigh. "It's not that big a deal, Kit."

"I agree. It wouldn't take more than a few hours of your time. So why are you balking?"

Irritated, Grant raked his fingers through his hair. "Just let it go, okay?"

"Look, I know you two don't exactly see eye to eye, but she's doing us a big favor here. Would it kill you to be nice and give her a tour?"

Planting his fists on his hips, he glared at her. "You are really stubborn, you know that?"

Kit mirrored his posture, and even though she was a good six inches shorter than him, she got as close to his face as she could. "It runs in the family," she shot back.

She stared him down until he threw up his hands in capitulation. "Okay, fine. I'll call her. Now will you lay off?"

"Absolutely." She gave him a sweet smile before issuing an additional instruction. "And be nice to her, okay? She's had a tough time."

Grant thought about the day he'd found Morgan slumped in the back of church, head bowed, cheeks stained with tears. He thought about her soul-baring confession when he'd offered a sympathetic ear. And he thought about the way he'd felt when he'd taken her hands in his. Kit's directive to be nice would be easy to follow. Too easy. And that scared him. A lot.

When Grant refocused on Kit, her eyes were curious. And way too perceptive. In general, he considered her empathy and insight to be assets. But not today. Because if she decided to delve into his heart, she might discover some things that surprised her. Things best kept hidden until he figured out how to deal with them.

There was only one problem.

He didn't even know where to start.

So he said a quick goodbye, sent Kit on her way, then turned to the only One who might be able to help him sort through his present dilemma.

Lord, life was already complicated before Morgan appeared, he prayed. *In fact, it was as complicated as I thought it could get. But I was wrong. More and more, I find my thoughts turning to her. But it's too soon. And we're too different. She's not the kind of woman I thought would ever appeal to me. Yet the more I see of her, the more I find myself attracted to her.*

Maybe it's just due to loneliness, Lord. Christine has been gone now for almost three years in everything but body. And I need some warmth in my life. Someone to share my days with. But I don't want to dishonor the memory of Christine and the special love we shared. Or make a mistake just because I yearn for the deep affection and tenderness I once knew. Please, Lord, guide me. Show me the right path. And give me the patience and strength to use restraint and take the time to discern Your will.

As Grant finished his prayer, he drew a deep, steadying breath. As always, he found·comfort in sharing his burdens with the Lord. And he knew his plea had been heard.

Which was a good thing. Because he also knew that every time he saw Morgan, it would be harder to resist her loveliness. And that he would only succeed with the help of a higher power.

Chapter Nine

Morgan surveyed her wardrobe with dismay. Grant had told her to dress warmly, in old clothes and to wear boots. The boots and the warmth she could manage, but she didn't have anything that qualified as old. Designer jeans and a cashmere turtleneck were about as close as she came, she decided, reaching for the items.

As Morgan dressed, she thought back to the conversation she'd had last night with Grant. Given his low profile since their encounter at church, she'd been surprised by his call. And even more surprised when he'd followed through on the camp tour suggestion, and invited her to drive out today.

Morgan had almost refused. Most of the promotional copy was finished. She'd even been able to incorporate some endorsements from prominent alumni, culled from the list Mary maintained. So she didn't feel a compelling need to see the camp in order to make the written appeal more effective. Besides, she doubted Grant was eager to act as her tour guide. Maybe Kit had said something to him, after all. Or perhaps he felt obligated to follow through, after more or less promising to do so at the board meeting.

But in the end she'd accepted his invitation—for purely selfish reasons. She enjoyed being with him, even if romance wasn't a possibility. He was a refreshing change from so many of the men she'd met in the advertising world, where form often took precedence over substance; where image was everything. With Grant, there was no pretense. He was what he seemed to be: an honest, caring, principled man who had his head on straight and whose values and priorities were in order. And she felt lucky that he'd crossed her path, if only for a few months. Because if there was one man like him, maybe there were others—who were more available.

Though for some reason that thought gave her little comfort.

A knock sounded on the door, and as Morgan rubbed her damp palms against her form-fitting jeans, she gave herself a stern reminder. We're just friends.

But even with that warning echoing in her mind, she couldn't rein in the sudden gallop of her heart when she opened the door. As usual, Grant looked fabulous. Casual clothes suited him, and the sheepskin-lined jacket, worn jeans that fit like a second skin and rugged boots just enhanced his already potent masculinity.

While Morgan did her quick assessment, Grant reciprocated, taking in the snug jeans that showed off her long legs to perfection and the black mock turtleneck that molded her soft curves. Her coppery hair framed her porcelain complexion, and her green eyes were spectacular.

Uncle Pete was right. She was a looker.

"Morning," she said, her voice a bit breathless.

He cleared his throat. "Good morning."

"Would you like some coffee before we leave?"

"No, thanks. We should get started, if you're ready. It's a long drive."

"Okay. Let me grab my coat."

She left the door open, and he took a cautious step inside, catching a fleeting whiff of the same faint, appealing fragrance he'd noticed before in her presence. As she started to shrug into her fleece-lined, quilted coat, he moved beside her and held the sleeves for her.

"Thanks," she murmured, noting with a sinking feeling that as soon as she had the coat on he stepped away and shoved his hands in his pockets. Maybe she should have declined his invitation, after all. The tension was vibrating in the air between them, which did not bode well for a relaxing day.

He turned to go, but when she hesitated he sent her a questioning look over his shoulder.

"Listen, Grant, if you have something else you need to do today, I understand. We don't have to visit the camp."

Indecision flickered in his eyes before he shook his head. "No. We should go. Sylvia was right. After all the work you've done, you should see the place. And Joe and Elizabeth are expecting us. I know she'll have prepared lunch."

"Okay. Then I'm ready."

He gave her a hand up into his truck, then climbed in beside her. As he guided the vehicle down Aunt Jo's narrow lane and pulled onto the road, she tried to think of something to talk about, something safe, that would ease the tension between them.

"At least it's a nice day," she offered.

"We're lucky. March can be pretty iffy up here. But this has been a mild winter overall."

"That's not exactly how I remember Christmas Eve."

A smile tugged at the corner of his mouth. "As I recall, we were in the midst of a pretty nasty storm. You just picked a bad day to arrive."

"Well, at last it's been better for the past three weeks. In fact, I've started start taking walks, as you suggested. And Kit has sent some work my way. Between that and job-hunting and working on the Good Shepherd campaign, I've been keeping pretty busy."

"By the way, every time I talk with one of the board members, they sing your praises. They can't believe you pulled off such stellar entertainment or lined up all those corporate sponsors."

"I'm glad something good came out of all those years of work."

"Still nothing on the job front, I take it?"

"No. I've broadened my search, though, so I'm hopeful that'll produce better results. But let's talk about something more pleasant today. Tell me a little more about the camp, and your experience there."

"It's a beautiful spot, right on the shores of Spruce Lake, not too far from Lewiston," he complied. "The first time I went, I had a sizeable chip on my shoulder. And I was feeling pretty sorry for myself. But after seeing some of the problems the other kids had, I soon realized that my situation was far better than just about anyone else's. It didn't take me long to see the light, realize how lucky I was—and clean up my act. The sessions are only a week long, but those seven days have a dramatic impact on a lot of kids. For me, it was a life-changing experience."

"And you went back the next year?"

"Yes. once you go, you have priority for subsequent years. So I went for the next four summers, and then I volunteered as a counselor for part of each summer while I was in school. I still help out for a week every year. In fact… that's where I met Christine."

Morgan looked over at Grant's strong profile and spoke in a quiet voice. "She must have been a very special woman."

A muscle twitched in his jaw before he responded. "She was. I was twenty-nine when I met her, and she was a couple of years younger. She taught school in Portland. I'd never believed in love at first sight, but think I knew from the moment I met her that someday we'd marry," he said softly. "We didn't rush things, though. We took time to get to know each other, and the more we learned, the more we realized how much we had in common."

Though he continued to look at the road ahead, Morgan knew he wasn't seeing the forested terrain around them, but the woman he loved. "She was very smart and very solid in her faith. She was also loving and gentle. She had a way of making everyone who came into contact with her feel important. I'm sure that's one of the reasons she was such a good teacher. Her students adored her, and she found great enjoyment in her work. But she was never obsessed with her career. She had a clear sense of priorities, and always put the people she loved first."

Unlike his mother, Morgan thought. And unlike her. At least until recent weeks.

When Grant grew silent, she sensed that he'd retreated to some private, inner world of memories that remained his only link to the woman who could no longer share them. Morgan waited a few moments before broaching her next question.

"Kit mentioned once that there was an accident," she prompted gently. "She said you were hiking?"

It seemed to take a few seconds for her question to register, and when it did Grant's jaw tensed. He swallowed hard before answering, and his voice wasn't quite steady when he spoke. "That's right. We both loved the outdoors, and we'd taken a weekend trip to Acadia National Park to celebrate our fourth anniversary. The scenery is spectacular, but it's also tough hiking. We were climbing up some rocks, and she…she slipped. I tried to grab her, but I…I didn't move fast enough."

As Grant struggled to hold on to his composure, his hands tightened on the wheel, whitening his knuckles.

"She called out to me when she started to fall. I grabbed for her, but she was too far away. I saw the fear in her eyes, and time seemed to stop for an instant as we looked at each other. The next thing I knew she was lying at the base of the rocks."

The image of Christine's crumpled, still form was forever etched in his mind, and the panic, anguish and terror he'd felt that day came rushing back with such intensity that, for a second, he couldn't breathe. He struggled for control, and when he continued, his tone was dispassionate, almost clinical, as if that was the only way he could get through this painful review of the accident that had changed his life forever.

"I remember scrambling down the rocks as fast as I could, then kneeling beside her and reaching for her wrist. And I remember thanking God when I felt a pulse. Her face was untouched, almost serene, and there were no visible signs of injury. But she'd fallen on her back, and I knew from the first-aid courses I'd taken as a camp instructor that back and head injuries were often more serious than they first appear. Fortunately, my cell phone was working, and I was able to call for help. But it took a long time for a rescue crew to arrive. An eternity. And I remember being overcome by this crushing, frustrating sense of helplessness. There was nothing I could do while I waited except hold Christine's hand and pray. Which I did, harder and more fervently than ever before in my life."

He cleared his throat and turned up the heat in the truck before he went on. "When we got the prognosis, I really didn't know what to expect. Christine had no serious damage except for the head injury, which had put her into a deep coma. The doctors said that wasn't uncommon in cases like hers, as the brain struggled to recover. But they couldn't tell me how long it would last. I just assumed that, in time, she would heal, and one day I'd walk in and find her waiting for me with that sparkling smile I loved. But that wasn't to be. It seemed God had other plans for us."

Morgan watched in silence as Grant's face contorted with pain. She yearned to reach out and offer him some sort of comfort, but she knew there was nothing she could say or do to ease the ache in his heart. Her throat constricted with emotion, and she dug in the pocket of her coat for a tissue, hoping to make a discreet dab at her eyes before Grant caught her in tears.

But luck was against her. He turned toward her just as she lifted a tissue to her face. "I'm sorry. I didn't mean to upset you," he apologized.

"It's a very sad story, Grant," she murmured. "I can't even begin to imagine how you coped with such a tragedy. Especially so early in your marriage. It would have broken a lot of people. Yet all that time, you were unwavering in your faithfulness and devotion. I admire that more than I can say."

"She would have done the same for me," he replied simply, dismissing her praise.

They fell silent then, but it wasn't the awkward, tense silence of earlier. It was a comfortable silence of reflection and ease. And that feeling lasted throughout the rest of the day.

When they arrived at the camp, Grant gave Morgan an extensive tour of the grounds, the buildings and the facilities strung along the rocky shore of the deep blue, pine-rimmed lake. He took her arm as they clambered over boulders and made their way down quiet trails cushioned by pine needles, always attentive, always staying close so she didn't stumble. Once, when she did lose her footing, his arm shot out to steady her, and as she looked into his eyes she saw the deep blue of the cloudless sky and the clear, cobalt lake reflected in them. She also saw them darken, felt an almost imperceptible tightening of his grip on her arm, making her breath catch in her throat. But then he abruptly turned away to point out a fir-studded island in the middle of the lake.

By the time they made their way back to the main lodge, Joe and Elizabeth were ready to welcome them for a homecooked meal. While Morgan savored the flavorful pot roast and the tender carrots and potatoes, the couple told her story after story about their experiences at Good Shepherd, putting a face on the people at the camp and giving it a life that Morgan had sensed, but not felt, from the brochure Grant had first sent her.

"Remember Ricky, Grant?" Elizabeth asked as she served up warm apple cobbler for dessert.

Grant had been quiet for much of the meal, but now he smiled. "How could I forget?"

"He was a pistol," Joe said with a laugh.

"Tell Morgan about him," Elizabeth encouraged Grant.

Grant hesitated. He'd been reluctant to make eye contact with Morgan since that unsettling moment in the woods, when he'd once again found himself drawn to her in ways that made him feel guilty—and disloyal to Christine. But he couldn't very well ignore Elizabeth's request. So he took a deep breath and turned to his guest.

"Ricky came to us the first time when he was about twelve," Grant told her. "Like a lot of the kids, he was from a troubled home. His father had deserted the family when he was two, and his mother was into the drug scene big-time. By twelve, he'd seen it all and was tough as nails. And he didn't want any part of Good Shepherd or the 'Jesus stuff,' as he called it.

"Anyway, his first night here, he ran away. Except he got lost. And all of the counselors had to go out searching for him in the woods."

"Including you," Elizabeth interjected. "How old were you then, Grant? Eighteen, maybe?"

"Yeah, I think so. I ended up finding him, huddled under a tree about a mile from camp, absolutely terrified. He'd never been away from the city, or in a place without any lights. The darkness freaked him out."

"Until you showed him the stars," Joe said.

A smile whispered at Grant's lips. "When I found him, I'm not sure if he was more scared of the dark or of the punishment for running away. But instead of getting mad, I gave him an astronomy lesson," he explained to Morgan.

That sounded like Grant. "Why do I think you made a friend for life?" she mused with an answering smile.

"He did," Joe confirmed. "After that, Ricky was Grant's shadow. And when the week ended, he didn't want to leave. He came back every summer for a number of years, always the week Grant was here. He told me once that if it hadn't been for Good Shepherd Camp, he'd have ended up dead in a street fight before he was twenty. But he found friends here. And support. And despite himself, God."

"Where is he now?" Morgan asked.

"He's an attorney in Boston," Elizabeth said with pride. "And he handles the youth ministry at his church."

"That's a remarkable story," Morgan said, impressed.

"It's just one of many," Grant replied. "That's why this fund-raiser is so important. There are still a lot of Rickys out there who need what Good Shepherd has to offer."

As they finished their coffee and Grant glanced at his watch, Morgan took the cue.

"I guess we need to head back. Elizabeth, Joe, thank you so much for your hospitality. And for the stories. I have a much better understanding now of the impact the camp has had on so many lives. And I also have some ideas on how to revise the text of the brochure to make it even more effective."

"We're so glad you came," Elizabeth said, rising to retrieve their coats. "You're welcome anytime."

The drive home was quiet. Grant seemed lost in thought, and Morgan had plenty to think about herself. Especially her tour guide. The more she saw of Grant, the more she liked him. But even if Christine wasn't in the picture—and that was a big *if*—there were still too many obstacles for a relationship between them to succeed. Grant was happy living on the back roads of Maine; Morgan was a big-city girl. Grant liked life in the slow lane; Morgan was on the fast track. Grant made time for family and causes in which he believed; until these past few weeks, Morgan hadn't had time for anything but work. But even though she had more balance in her life now, and a better perspective, she and Grant were still very different.

And Christine's shadow was too long.

When they pulled up in front of Jo's cottage, Grant came around to help Morgan out of the high cab of his truck. His hands were strong and steady, and once again Morgan's pulse accelerated at his touch. But she stifled her feelings as best she could. She needed to keep her distance. For both their sakes. Neither needed the kind of complications that romance would bring.

Morgan disengaged her hands from his and moved a couple of steps away before she turned to him. "Thank you for the tour, Grant. I'm sorry it took up most of your day."

"Sylvia was right. It was important for you to see Good Shepherd. I have more time on my hands now, anyway."

Because Christine is gone.

He didn't say it. But he didn't have to. Morgan could read it in his eyes. Along with wrenching pain and a desolate loneliness.

Morgan could relate to that. She'd been feeling more and more lonely herself over the past few weeks. Forgetting her resolve of moments before, she stepped closer again and laid her hand on his arm.

"I want you to know how sorry I am about… about everything," she said softly. "And I just want you to know how much I respect you. And how much I envy your strength. I wish I had even half of it."

As Grant gazed into Morgan's sincere, compassionate eyes, he suddenly didn't feel strong at all. He felt lost. And alone. And needy.

Grant had always had tremendous self-control and discipline. And those traits had held him in good stead over the past few years. But he'd lived in an emotional vacuum way too long, and as he savored Morgan's lovely face, those virtues seemed to desert him. His mouth went dry, and he was filled with a yearning to reach out and touch her porcelain skin, run his fingers through her shiny, copper hair, taste her inviting lips. The impulse was so strong that he had started to reach for her before he realized that things were getting out of control.

With an abrupt movement, he yanked his hand back and jammed it into the pocket of his sheepskin jacket.

"I need to go," he said in a curt, clipped manner.

Morgan was startled, though not surprised, by his sudden retreat. And she was more than a little disappointed, because even though her head told her that it wouldn't be wise to get involved with Grant, her heart said otherwise.

"I'll see you around, I guess." She couldn't stop the tremor that rippled through her voice.

He gave a brusque nod, climbed into his truck and pulled away.

And he didn't look back.

He didn't dare.

Because he was afraid the tenuous hold he had on his self control would snap as easily as a dry, lifeless twig too long deprived of water if he allowed himself one more look at her face.

But it took every ounce of his will power to keep his gaze fixed on the road ahead instead of on the woman he'd left behind.

Morgan pulled her sporty car into a parking place in front of the barnlike structure that bore the name Kincaid Woodworks and set her brake. She hadn't seen Grant since he'd given her a tour of the camp, and considering their parting, she hadn't intended to seek him out. But she had good news, and she figured he could use some cheering up after all he'd been through. So she'd decided to pay him an impromptu visit.

As she entered the tiny reception area in the front of the building, the muffled sounds of a saw and the smell of newly planed wood greeted her. A button was mounted on the wall, next to a sign inviting customers to "ring bell for service." She pressed it, only to be startled by the loud clang that echoed through the building. It sounded much like the bell that had been used to signal the end of recess in grade school, she recalled with a nervous grin.

The saw went silent, and Andrew came through the door from the back room.

"Morgan! It's good to see you," he greeted her, extending a hand. "You've been keeping yourself pretty scarce."

She returned his firm grip. "I haven't wandered far from the cottage," she admitted. "Is Grant around?"

"Last time I checked he was behind the shop, inspecting a new load of maple. Shall I send him up, or would you like to go back?"

"I'll go back. I've never seen the workshop before."

As she followed Grant's father through the door marked Private, she glanced around with interest at the spacious shop. The pleasant scent of fresh-cut wood was much stronger back here, and various pieces of furniture in different stages of completion stood about. Grant had come back inside, and she spotted him in the far corner, intent on his work and oblivious to their approach. She watched as he leaned close to examine the front of the cabinet he was working on, and when he reached over to let his strong, lean fingers glide over the smooth surface, Morgan's pulse went haywire.

"Grant, you have a visitor."

He looked up, and for a moment he seemed taken aback by Morgan's presence. Caution warred with warmth in his eyes as he greeted her. "Hi. What brings you here?"

"I have something to show you. You might want to see this, too, Andrew." Morgan tried for an easy, conversational tone as she struggled to make her uncooperative lungs behave.

Setting aside a white bakery bag, she opened a folder, then pulled out two sheets of paper and handed them to Grant while Andrew looked over his son's shoulder. "You mentioned when we went to the camp that a reporter from Boston had called after I sent them some info on the benefit. So I started monitoring the paper on the Internet. This story appeared this morning."

As Grant and Andrew scanned the feature article, complete with pictures of the camp, Morgan pointed out that the reporter had used the backgrounder she'd created to contact not only Grant, as chairman, but some of the prominent alumni of the camp, as well. Comments from them were included, along with a quote from the featured entertainer for the event.

"It's a very positive article, and when I spoke with Mary this morning she said she'd already received quite a few phone calls about tickets, as well as inquiries from people who were interested in supporting the camp."

Grant looked over at her. Warmth had triumphed over caution in his eyes. And the effect of his smile registered at about an eight on the Richter scale. "This is fantastic! You really know your stuff, Morgan."

She flushed at his compliment. "You just need a hook to get reporters interested, and our stellar entertainment and successful alumni did the trick." She reached for the bakery bag and waved it under their noses. "And I brought some cookies to celebrate. Courtesy of the lo-cal bakery."

"Anybody home?"

They all turned at the sound of Kit's voice, and Andrew motioned her over. "Come and see what Morgan just brought in."

Kit joined them and perused the article. "Way to go, girl!" she congratulated Morgan when she finished. "With this kind of publicity, I expect the dinner will be a huge success. Bill and I are really looking forward to it, not only because it's a great cause, but it will be the social event of the season—make that the decade!—for us. The last time Bill wore a tux was at our wedding! You'll have to rent one, too, Grant."

"It's on my list of things to do."

Kit turned from Grant to Morgan. "So…who are you bringing?"

"Bringing?"

"Aren't you going to invite a date?"

Morgan shook her head. "Everybody I know is in Boston. It's too long a drive from there to Portland, especially since the event will run late."

Her expression innocent—maybe too innocent—Kit turned to Grant. "Why don't you two go together?"

Based on Grant's frown, the idea didn't appeal to him. Morgan stifled a pang of disappointment and spoke before he could respond. "I'm used to attending events by myself, Kit," she assured the other woman. "I did it all the time in Boston. My job required me to show up at lots of different kinds of social gatherings. I'm an old pro at going solo."

"I'm sure you are, but there's no need in this case," Kit countered. "You and Grant are both going. And it's a long drive by yourself, especially in the dark. Bill and I would be happy to take you, but we're going to make a night of it and stay until Sunday."

"I think Kit's idea makes a lot of sense, Grant," Andrew concurred.

When Grant's frown deepened, Morgan decided that was her cue to exit. "Look, we can sort all this out later. The event is still weeks away. In the meantime, I need to run. I'll just let myself out. See you all later."

And before anyone could say another word, she made a hasty escape.

After watching her leave, Grant met the disapproving eyes of his sister. Her critical expression was mirrored by his father. He planted his fists on his hips and glared at them. "What?"

Kit wasn't about to be intimidated. "You weren't very nice to Morgan. She doesn't know that many people up here. The least you could do is take her to the dinner, after all the work she's put into it. I think you hurt her feelings."

"Kit's right, son," Andrew agreed.

"Look, I'm not in the mood for social events

right now, okay?" Grant raked his fingers through his hair, feeling cornered. "I even considered not attending the dinner, but as chairman of the board, I think I have to go. I didn't mean to hurt Morgan's feelings, but I'm not very good company at the moment."

"You're better than no company," Kit shot back.

"I'm not so sure of that." His shoulders slumped and he leaned back against the cabinet, jamming his hands into his pockets. "I'm barely getting through the days right now," he admitted, his eyes downcast. When he continued speaking, his voice was rough at the edge. "It's a struggle to adjust and to accept that…that Christine is gone. I'll think about what you said, but I just need some time."

Kit's eyes grew soft, and she glanced at Andrew as she reached out to put a hand on Grant's arm. "I'm sorry for coming on so strong. I know how hard this is for you, and I'm sure Morgan understands." She turned to Andrew. "I brought some lunch for everybody. Is Uncle Pete around?"

"He's out back. I'll get him."

"I baked your favorite brownies," Kit told Grant.

"Thanks. I'll be right over."

He watched her walk away, grateful she'd backed off. Even though her suggestion made sense, he wasn't sure it was a good idea. For all the reasons he'd laid out. As well as for the ones he hadn't.

His attraction to Morgan. And his guilt about it.

Grant didn't understand why he was drawn to Morgan. But he knew it was much too soon to have those kinds of feelings. And he didn't have the energy to deal with disturbing emotions and difficult questions right now.

So taking her to the black-tie dinner, which required a long drive to and from Portland with just each other for company, was not a good idea.

Chapter Ten

"Anybody home?"

Grant came out from behind the bookcase he was sanding and smiled at Bill. "Hi. What's up?"

"Your sister sent me on a mission of mercy. Homemade cookies." Bill held up a large plastic container.

Grinning, Grant wiped his hands on his jeans. "Perfect timing. I was just about ready for a break. Do you want to join me?"

Bill checked his watch. "Well, I'm on my way to a meeting…but Kit's chocolate-chip-pecan cookies are hard to resist. So, okay, I'll give in to temptation," he capitulated with a smile, as he followed Grant to the lunchroom in the corner of the shop. "Where are Andrew and Pete?"

"Making a delivery," Grant told him as he reached for the coffeepot on the counter.

"Which is a good thing. The last time someone brought cookies, those two devoured most of them before I could grab more than a couple. Turnabout is fair play."

Bill took a seat and opened the container. "I thought Kit was your sole cookie source. Who's infringing on her territory?"

A shadow passed over Grant's eyes as he set their mugs on the worn wooden surface and joined Bill at the table. "Morgan brought cookies the other day."

"No kidding? That was nice. I heard about the coverage Good Shepherd got in the Boston paper, by the way. That was great."

"Yeah. She's good at what she does."

"She's a hard worker, that's for sure. We found that out on Christmas. Remember how she had to excuse herself during dinner to return those calls?"

"I remember."

"But Kit was just saying the other day how much Morgan has mellowed since she's been here. And I have to agree. She doesn't seem nearly as driven or high-strung."

"Yeah."

As he sipped his coffee, Bill studied his brother-in-law over the rim of the mug. "So how much longer will she be in Seaside?"

"I guess until a better offer comes along."

"How do you feel about that?"

"What do you mean?"

"She's a nice woman."

"I know."

"Kit will miss her. And...I have a feeling you will, too."

Taken aback, Grant wrapped his hands around the large, no-nonsense mug. Even though he'd never given voice to his feelings about Morgan, somehow Bill seemed to have picked up on them. Maybe that wasn't a bad thing. Grant needed to talk with someone, and he'd always valued his brother-in-law's insights and counsel. Maybe Bill could help him sort out his jumbled thoughts and feelings.

"I will," he ventured.

"Have you told her that?"

Slowly Grant shook his head.

"Why not?"

A troubled frown creased Grant's brow. "Because it's wrong to feel this way."

"What way?"

Grant raked his fingers through his hair. "I'm not even sure I can talk about this. I feel guilty enough already."

"Guilt isn't necessarily a bad thing, when it works in tandem with our conscience," Bill remarked. "But sometimes it can be misplaced. Sometimes, instead of stopping us from doing things we shouldn't do, it can keep us from doing things we should do. Could this be one of those times?"

Grant's frown deepened. "I don't know."

"Do you want to talk it through? Sometimes that helps."

"I thought you had a meeting to go to."

"Actually, it's a tea that the ladies' guild is sponsoring. I promised to put in an appearance. But to be honest, I'd rather eat Kit's cookies. And talk to you," Bill confessed with a grin. "As long as I show up for a few minutes, they'll be happy."

After flashing him a brief answering smile, Grant's face grew somber and he stared into the murky depths of his coffee. "I like Morgan," he acknowledged. "A lot. Too much, in fact."

"How much is too much?"

A warm flush crept up the back of his neck, and Grant shifted in his seat. "There have been a few times when we've been together that I've been…very attracted to her. And when I drove her home last week, after the tour of Good Shepherd, I almost…I wanted to…to touch her."

"She's a lovely woman," Bill replied.

"But Christine's barely been gone three months, Bill. I loved her! I shouldn't feel this way!" The conflict in Grant's heart was reflected in his eyes.

"She's really been gone a lot longer than that, Grant," Bill reminded him gently. "Almost three years. You've been alone a long time."

"But I loved her!" Grant repeated, his voice anguished.

"I know you did. You two had a wonderful marriage. And your loyalty and faithfulness and devotion to her after the accident, long after all of us had given up hope of her recovery, was an inspiration to everyone. You have nothing to feel guilty about. If anything, you're to be commended. I think your diligence and commitment these past three years is best summed up in scripture—well done, good and faithful servant."

Doubt clouded Grant's eyes. "Even if that's true, it seems too soon to have such strong feelings for someone else."

"You know, the Lord works in mysterious ways," Bill observed, his expression thoughtful. "Morgan came into your life at this point for a reason, Grant. Just as Christine left it at this point for a reason. I've thought about the timing myself, and it occurred to me that maybe

God left Christine with you so you wouldn't be alone while you waited for a special woman to come along who would fill your heart with love. And when she did, the Lord called Christine home."

Jolted, Grant stared at Bill. Could he be right? Was this all part of God's plan?

"In my heart, I also know that Christine wouldn't have wanted you to mourn forever," Bill continued. "She was a warm, giving woman who understood the value and importance of love. She wouldn't have wanted you to be alone."

Maybe that was true, Grant conceded. It would be in keeping with Christine's generous nature. But how could he be sure? "I'd like to think you're right," he replied.

"Pray on it," Bill suggested. "Open your heart to God's guidance. That's who I turn to when I'm confused. And He always comes through, if we listen for His voice." Bill took a last sip of his coffee, then stood and placed a hand on the younger man's shoulders. "Putting my vocation aside for a moment, may I tell you something as a friend? Morgan is an extraordinary woman. I'd think long and hard about letting her walk away."

Grant's face grew bleak. "I may not be able

to stop her even if I try. She comes from a different world, Bill. And even though she's changed a lot, I have a feeling that world still has appeal for her. When the right offer comes along, I think she'll leave."

Bill gazed at him steadily. "Maybe you could make an offer that would change her mind."

Grant didn't know how to respond to that. So he remained silent.

"Think about it," Bill advised, squeezing his shoulder.

As Grant watched Bill leave, he lifted his mug and took a sip. Ever since he'd first experienced an attraction to Morgan, he'd worked hard to stifle it because of the guilt that had overwhelmed him. But all at once his heart felt lighter. Bill didn't think his feelings were inappropriate. In fact, he'd encouraged him to pursue them. Had suggested that Morgan might be willing to remain in Seaside if the right offer came along. An offer only Grant could make.

Grant wasn't sure Bill was right. But most of the time his brother-in-law's insights were on target. So perhaps there was a chance that things could turn out well after all. He wasn't ready to take such a bold step yet. But perhaps, in time, he would be.

And suddenly Grant experienced an emotion that had long been in short supply in his life.

Hope.

Morgan dialed A.J's number and strolled over to the bay window to look at the sea. Her sister answered on the fourth ring, sounding a bit breathless.

"A.J.? Did I catch you at a bad time?"

"Morgan? No. I just got out of the shower, so I had to make a mad dash for the phone."

"Shall I call you back later?"

"No, I'm fine. So to what do I owe the honor of this call?"

"Do I have to have a reason for calling?"

"No. But you usually do."

Her sister was right, Morgan acknowledged. But that was in the past. She intended to make some changes, starting today. "I just called to chat."

There was a brief silence on the other end as A.J. digested this news. "For real?"

"Yeah. For real."

"Cool! So how's life in the boonies?"

"We do have running water here, you know," Morgan informed her with a grin.

"I hear the electricity is iffy, though."

"Very funny. Actually, life here is okay. I'm

standing at the window right now enjoying the view of the sea. It's an incredible blue, and the sky is filled with huge, puffy clouds. I can see why Aunt Jo liked this place so much."

Again, there were a few beats of silence before A.J. spoke. "It sounds great. And I'm glad you're taking the time to notice. So are you a lady of leisure today? I remember when you used to work on Sundays."

"Those days are past. Other than church this morning, I have no plans for the day, except maybe a long walk."

This time, the silence stretched even longer. "Are you sure this is Morgan Williams, formerly of Boston, sister of A.J. and Clare? The workaholic career woman?"

"Former workaholic," Morgan corrected her.

"Well, praise the Lord! It sounds like you've finally seen the light."

"I guess you could say that. But it took some pretty dramatic events before the message sank in. At first, I thought losing my job was a catastrophe."

"And you don't now?"

"Let's just say I have a different perspective. I still love my work, and Kit—Grant's sister—has been sending some small jobs my way, so I'm keeping my skills fresh. Plus, the Good

Shepherd project is huge, which helps, too. But I guess I've come to realize there are other, more important things in life."

"I'm happy for you, Morgan. I've been praying for this day."

"Looks like your prayers were heard."

"So what are your plans? Are you still job-hunting?"

"Yes. I have to have some kind of income. But the jobs I've gotten through Kit will tide me over until something turns up."

"So you don't have any immediate plans to leave Maine, even though you've met the four-week residency stipulation?"

"No. Where would I go? At least I have some work here—which is more than I have anywhere else."

"Hey, maybe if you're still there when our six-month assignments from Aunt Jo are over, Clare and I can come visit."

"It would be nice for the three of us to get together," Morgan agreed.

"Yeah. We missed you at Christmas. But at least Grant's family adopted you for the day, so you weren't alone. How is he doing, by the way?"

Morgan's eyes softened in sympathy. "I think he's having a rough time."

"That's understandable," A.J. reasoned. "What a terrible tragedy."

"He has a very strong faith, so I'm sure that helps a lot."

"It does." A.J.'s prompt reply reminded Morgan that her sister spoke from experience. "But it also helps to know others care." Then she shifted to a more upbeat tone. "So can I assume that I'll be hearing from you more in the future?"

"I think that's a safe bet. How are things going with the bookshop?"

A.J. chuckled. "That's a subject for a whole separate conversation."

"Are you trying to give me an incentive to call again soon?"

"Yeah. Is it working?"

"As a matter of fact, yes," Morgan said, laughing. "I'll call you next week, okay?"

"Sounds good to me. And Morgan...welcome back to the fold."

As Morgan replaced the receiver, a gentle smile tugged at the corners of her mouth. A.J.'s spontaneous, upbeat attitude had sometimes bothered the old Morgan, who thought her younger sister was out of touch with the real world of fast-paced business.

But as Morgan had learned over the past few

weeks, she had been the one out of touch with all the things that mattered most. The lesson hadn't been easy to learn. It had taken a radical shake-up in her world to put her on the right track. Now that she was on it, however, she was determined not to lose her way again.

It would be a challenge, though. Here in Maine, surrounded by people who had their priorities straight, who took time to smell the flowers along the way, the lesson was easy to remember. Back in the big city, it would be tougher.

Maybe that was why Aunt Jo had loved this cottage so much, Morgan speculated. Her great-aunt had been a businesswoman—albeit not as driven as Morgan—and running a business took its toll. Maybe she had come here to renew and refresh. Not a bad plan, except Morgan had no idea what she and Grant would do with the cottage once the six months were over. He owned half of it. She couldn't expect him to maintain it just for her occasional use.

She supposed they'd have to discuss it soon. Although it probably wasn't high on his priority list at the moment, she acknowledged.

Casting a glance at the calendar in the kitchen, she noted that the Good Shepherd board meeting was in ten days. It was unlikely she'd see Grant before then. But A.J.'s words echoed in her mind. "It helps to know others care." Morgan knew that Grant's family had rallied around him more than ever since Christine died. But it couldn't hurt for her to extend a hand of caring and friendship. Maybe after the meeting, she'd follow his example and offer to buy him a cup of coffee, as he had once done for her.

In the meantime, she needed to think of just the right way to phrase the invitation. It had to come across as warm and friendly, but not intrusive or pushy. Just one friend extending a caring hand to another.

For someone who wrote ad copy every day, she figured it should be a piece of cake.

By the time the day of the meeting rolled around, Morgan had finely honed the exact phrasing of her invitation.

Except Grant didn't show up.

Instead, Sylvia took his place at the head of the table and called the meeting to order. "Let's get started, everyone. Grant called me last night and asked that I preside. He had to have emergency arthroscopic surgery on his knee yesterday, but he's home and doing okay. He apologizes for his absence, especially with the fund-raising drive in full swing, but I assured him we understood and promised to give him a full report after the meeting. John, will you start us off with a prayer?"

As they bowed their heads, Morgan only half listened to the minister's words. Her thoughts were on Grant instead. For the next two hours, she did her best to focus on Good Shepherd business, but as soon as the meeting was over she headed back toward Seaside, making a quick stop at the one restaurant in town that was open in the off season. Even though arthroscopic surgery wasn't that invasive, she was sure Grant would be laid up for a couple of days. It would be a nice gesture to drop off a meal from the local café.

Morgan had never been to Grant's house before, but he'd given her his address and home phone number when she'd first arrived, and she'd recorded them in her pocket organizer. She dug it out of her purse now, and asked the woman at the restaurant for directions to his street.

As Morgan made her way through the village, it occurred to her that she had never made a conscious decision to visit Grant. It had been an automatic, reflexive response—much like a knee jerk induced by the tapping of a rubber hammer. But as she approached his street, she grew uncertain.

Slowing the car, she considered retreating. But she'd already bought the food. And she couldn't be more than a block or two from his house. So she might as well follow through. If he didn't want visitors, she'd just drop off her care package and leave.

A couple of minutes later, she pulled up in front of his house, a tiny bungalow on the outskirts of the town, set back from the road amid a grove of pine trees. The clapboard siding was painted a light gray color, and sky-blue shutters framed the windows. The house and grounds were meticulous, Morgan noted, as she pulled into the driveway and parked behind his truck.

For a couple of minutes she just sat there. Then, taking a deep breath, she reached for the bag and headed toward the door before her nerve deserted her.

Morgan pressed the door bell, finding some reassurance in the lovely tole-painted welcome sign that hung on the front door. She suspected that it had been placed there by Christine, and she hoped the message still held true.

As the seconds ticked by with no response, Morgan pressed the bell again. Since his truck was in the driveway, she was sure Grant was home. But maybe he was confined to bed and unable to get to the door. She supposed she could try the back door, or ring him from her cell phone, or…

Suddenly the door was pulled open, and Grant, balanced on crutches, looked at her in surprise.

"Sylvia told us about your surgery. I figured you'd be laid up for a couple of days, so I wanted to drop off a care package." Morgan held up the white sack, which was emitting enticing aromas.

Grant eyed it hungrily. "Is that by any chance the lasagna special from the café in town?"

"None other."

He moved aside, wielding the awkward crutches as best he could, and swung the door wider. "Come in, oh bringer of food!"

"Just point me to your kitchen," Morgan said as she stepped across the threshold.

He gestured toward the back of the house. "It's not hard to find. Christine and I used to joke that someone with long enough arms could reach just about anything in this place if they stood in the middle of the living room."

Morgan gave the house a swift perusal as she made her way to the tiny efficiency kitchen. Grant wasn't kidding. The bungalow was minuscule. The living room, dining area and kitchen were just one long, open room that ran the entire length of the right side of the house. A small hall branched off to the left, where she assumed the bedrooms were—if there was more than one. She noticed a photo of Aunt Jo on a tiny table as she passed, and she paused to look at it.

"That was taken at the cottage a couple of years ago," Grant offered.

Morgan lifted the silver frame and studied her aunt's face. Though nearly eighty, she looked far younger. Her eyes were alive and vibrant, her smile warm and welcoming.

"She looks happy," Morgan commented.

"She was. The cottage was her haven. She was always relaxed and at peace there."

With sudden remorse, Morgan wished she'd taken time to get to know her great-aunt better. But regrets wouldn't change the past. All she could do was focus on the future—an attitude she had a feeling Aunt Jo would approve of. And even if Morgan hadn't known Aunt Jo as well as she would have liked, the older woman—through her bequest—had still influenced her great-niece's life, changed it for the better. And for that Morgan was grateful.

"So how about that food?" Grant prompted hopefully.

Morgan turned to him with a grin. "Hungry, are we?"

"You might say that."

She put the picture back on the table and walked toward the kitchen. As she removed the disposable container from the bag, Grant maneuvered himself toward a chair. "Can you stay a few minutes?"

"I didn't plan to make this a social call."

"It's nice to have some company," he assured her. "It's been pretty quiet around here for the past couple of days. Dad and Uncle Pete have their hands full at the shop with me out of commission, and the twins have the flu, so Kit has been busy nursing them."

She busied herself setting out the food, debating whether to stay. In the end, she gave into the temptation. "Okay. What would you like to drink?"

"I think that's my line."

"Not today."

"Thanks," he acceded with a smile. "There's soda in the refrigerator. Help yourself to one, too."

While she retrieved the drinks, he lowered himself carefully into a chair.

"That looks painful," she sympathized.

"It's not that bad," he replied with a dismissive shrug.

"So what happened?"

"I think I mentioned when you first arrived that I'd slipped on the ice a few years back. Well, I injured the cartilage then and, in hindsight, probably should have had it fixed right away. But I figured I could live with it. Then, last week, I twisted it again when Dad and I were moving a large breakfront. That pretty much finished off the ligament and locked up my knee. In my business, immobility is a problem. The good news is my orthopedic surgeon is an old school friend, and he got me in on an emergency basis. I should be up and around in a few days."

He tackled the food with gusto while Morgan sipped her soda and took in the homey touches throughout the cottage. "You have a nice place."

"It has a lot of happy memories. But it doesn't have a great water view, like Jo's cottage. And it's too small. Christine and I never intended to stay here forever. Once we had children…" His voice trailed off and his hand stilled. Then, with an obvious effort, he made himself continue eating. "Anyway, at some point I expect I'll sell it. So how did the board meeting go?"

"Fine. Mary said the invitations went out ten days ago, and they're generating a good response. The dinner should be a huge success."

At the mention of the dinner, Grant's brow furrowed. Kit's suggestion that he take Morgan had been on his mind a lot. But he was still hesitant. "Look, about the dinner…"

"Hey, Grant, it's okay," she cut him off. "I know Kit meant well, but I've gone to hundreds of those kinds of events alone. It's no big deal. So don't worry about it. By the way, I've also managed to line up some more coverage in area newspapers, in addition to the story in Boston."

Her rapid change of subject made it clear that she didn't want to discuss the dinner, and Grant was relieved. "That's great. You've done a fabulous job. And speaking of jobs…any news?"

"Not yet."

"But you're still looking?" At her nod, he speared another bite of his lasagna. "I know Kit's been sending work your way. I thought maybe you'd like the freelance life."

"It has its pluses. But I'm not sure I could make enough of an income just freelancing."

"How much is enough?"

"Enough to live on."

He reached for a piece of garlic bread and took a bite. "I guess it does take a lot of money to maintain the kind of life you lived in Boston."

"Or just about anywhere."

"Not necessarily. It depends on your needs. It doesn't take a lot of resources to lead a simple life."

She propped her chin in her hand. "Like yours, you mean. But even you need to make a living, Grant."

"True. But I don't need to be rich. At least not in a monetary sense. Making a lot of money has never been one of my goals."

"You make me feel mercenary."

He grew contrite. "Then I apologize. Especially since you're here on a mission of mercy. And after you've given so much of your time to the Good Shepherd project." He shrugged. "Maybe there's a way to blend worldly success with simple values. I just never figured out how to do it. Nor did I want to." A yawn snuck up on him, and he gave her a sheepish look. "Sorry about that. I didn't sleep very well last night."

"No apology necessary. Go get some rest." She stood and reached for the empty lasagna container and soda can.

"I can clean that up later," he protested.

"It's already done. Can I do anything else for you before I leave?"

The swift darkening of his eyes made her heart hammer in her chest, and she turned away to rummage for her keys. By the time she looked back at him, his eyes were shuttered.

"I'll let myself out," she told him, hoping he wouldn't notice the breathless quality of her voice.

"Okay. Thanks again for stopping by."

"No problem."

She made her way to the front door without delay, feeling anxious and off balance. She'd hesitated about coming over, afraid she might disturb Grant. But instead, he'd disturbed her.

With a look that had affected her in ways she didn't want to think about.

And with his simple but fundamental question about money: "How much is enough?"

Grant's probing question, his sincere convictions about his way of life, and his deep contentment made her wonder if a big-city job was what she wanted after all. Could she be content with a simpler life?

Morgan wasn't sure yet. But she was beginning to suspect that she could be.

Especially if she shared it with the right man.

* * *

"Morgan, do you have a minute?"

At the sound of Bill Adams's voice, Morgan stopped and glanced back toward the church door. The minister said something to the woman he'd been talking to, then made his way over to Morgan.

"I'm glad I caught you. I have a favor to ask. I don't know if you've paid much attention to the teen program we have, but now and then we like to bring in speakers to talk about their careers. It's good to expose young people to a lot of options as they plan their futures. We've never invited anyone from the advertising or marketing field before, and I wondered if you'd be willing to address the group. It's a very informal session, and we like to allow lots of Q-and-A time. So you wouldn't need to prepare much."

Morgan had spoken to college classes before, and she still had all of her notes. So it would be easy to accommodate Bill's request. "Sure. When do you want me to do this?"

"Would two weeks from Wednesday work? That way, we can publicize it in the bulletin for the next couple of Sundays."

"No problem. My calendar isn't nearly as full as it was when I lived in Boston," she said with a smile.

"Are you saying that you lead a dull and boring life here in rural Maine?" he asked, grinning.

"No. In fact, I'm enjoying it. I can see why Aunt Jo loved it here. And I think Serenity Point is an apt name for her cottage. It's very calm and peaceful there."

"It's a great spot," he agreed. "So I'll put you down for April 17. We meet at seven, at the town hall. The meetings are open to all the teens from the area, so there could be a good turnout."

"I'll be there."

As Morgan turned to go, she caught a glimpse of Grant exiting the church. When he noticed her, he raised a hand in greeting, and she responded. Their paths hadn't crossed since she'd stopped by his cottage, so she was glad to note that he was now walking without crutches.

She considered going back to speak with him, then thought better of it. She liked Grant. Too much. And he seemed to like her. But even though he was technically available now, she knew his heart still belonged to Christine. Maybe it always would. And even if he did one day find a way to open his heart to love with someone new, she wasn't his type. Any attraction he felt for her was surely being triggered by nothing more than loneliness.

So it was better if they kept their distance. Wasn't it?

Chapter Eleven

"Grant? I need your help."

Grant speared a forkful of broccoli from his microwave dinner and shifted the phone against his ear. "What's up, Kit?"

"I was supposed to take the girls to the town hall tonight for the teen session. You know, the one where Morgan is going to speak about her career? Anyway, Bill went to Brunswick for a meeting, and his car died. So I need to go get him. I don't think I'll be back in time to take the girls. If you could drop them off, we can pick them up later."

"Sure. What time?"

"They need to be there by seven."

Grant checked his watch. He still wasn't used to eating dinner this early, but since he wasn't visiting Christine over lunch anymore, he was able to leave the shop at a more reasonable hour. "No problem. Tell them I'll be by at quarter till."

"Thanks. You're a lifesaver!"

"Remember that the next time I need a favor," he teased.

Forty-five minutes later, when Grant pulled up in front of Kit's house, the girls were waiting. As they clambered into his truck, he grinned at their excited chatter. "You two seem pretty wound up."

"This is going to be cool!" Nancy said.

"Yeah," Nicki chimed in. "Morgan is a lot of fun. And Mom told me about her neat job in Boston. Did you know she's been to Europe? Several times! And her company paid her way!"

"And she's met a bunch of famous people," Nancy added.

"A lot of kids from school are coming tonight," Nicki told him. "Are you staying?"

"I thought this was just for teens."

"It is. But lots of times the parents stay in the back, if we have a good speaker," Nancy explained. "I think there will be a bunch of adults there tonight."

"You should stay, Uncle Grant," Nicki urged him. "Morgan still doesn't know that many people around here, and she'd probably like to see a friendly face in the audience."

Grant wasn't so sure Morgan would consider his face to be friendly. Not after he'd side-stepped Kit's suggestion that he take her to the Good Shepherd dinner. Of course, that hadn't stopped her from delivering the hot meal to his house a couple of weeks before. So maybe she didn't hold his less-than-enthusiastic response against him.

And he *was* curious about what she'd say. He'd suspected she knew prominent people, based on her ability to line up such stellar entertainment for the Good Shepherd dinner. But he'd had no idea about the trips to Europe. And there must be a lot of other things about her job he didn't know. He'd been so turned off by her obsession with it, and by the demands it made, that he hadn't allowed himself to believe that it might have some appealing aspects. Maybe if he knew more about what she'd done in Boston, he would better understand why she'd focused on her work to the exclusion of everything else. And why she wanted to return to that world, albeit it with a different perspective.

Come to think of it, maybe it would be interesting to see what kind of picture she painted of her career. Morgan certainly didn't seem like the same person he'd talked with by phone months ago, when she'd asked him to meet with her on Christmas Eve. But he could be wrong. Maybe her presentation tonight would give him a clue as to whether she'd undergone any fundamental change.

Not that it mattered, of course. Even if she had, even if she'd realigned her priorities, he was pretty sure that Seaside, Maine, was not where she intended to stay. He figured she regarded her time here as a brief sojourn, an opportunity to regroup and regain perspective. And he was fairly certain she'd accomplished that.

He was also sure that one of these days, Morgan Williams would leave just as unexpectedly as she'd come. It would just take the right offer. And now that he'd seen her diligent and creative work on the Good Shepherd project, and heard Kit sing her praises for the freelance jobs she'd done, he knew such an offer wasn't a matter of if.

It was a matter of when.

So, even if circumstances were different, even if he one day felt ready to give love another chance, even if he thought that the attraction between them could lead to something deeper and more substantive, that was a major problem.

His life was here.

And it always would be.

Morgan gave her notes one final review as she waited to be introduced. It had been awhile since she'd addressed a group of young people, and she was looking forward to it. They tended to be an eager, interested audience, hungry for knowledge of the so-called glamorous world she inhabited, and in the past, she'd always painted a rosy and appealing picture. But she'd added some new content to her presentation over the past week, because it was important for young people to understand the expectations of careers they might choose—including what they would be asked to give up. When she finished tonight, they might still be awed by the glamour and prestige, but at least they'd have a more balanced, realistic view of the sacrifices required to achieve them.

She looked up and caught the eyes of Nancy and Nicki in the audience of about fifty teenagers. They waved, and she smiled and raised her hand in response. A number of adults lingered in the back of the room, and she wondered if they planned to stay for her talk. Though she scanned the group, hoping to spot Kit or Bill, she saw neither.

But she did see Grant.

He was talking to an older man, and her heart flip-flopped as she stared at his strong, appealing profile. It had never occurred to her that he would be here. And it rattled her. She knew he'd been turned off by her obsession with work and unimpressed by her priorities when they'd met. So why did he want to hear about her career now?

Morgan didn't have time to ponder that question, because the director of the youth ministry had risen and was introducing her. So she forced her thoughts back to the presentation. Just ignore him, she told herself. Focus on the teenagers. Don't look at the back of the room.

And that's exactly what she did. For the next forty-five minutes, she told the young people about her trips to Europe, the black-tie dinners she'd attended and the celebrities she'd met. But she also told them about the long hours, the frustrations, the politics and the stress. She tempered the glitz and the excitement with the cold, hard realties of corporate life: the uncertainties, the intense competition, the sometimes unreasonable demands.

"So it's a great career in a lot of ways," she

finished. "But bear in mind, if you have your sights set on big-time success in a major market, you'll have to give up a lot to attain it. However, there are also less stressful ways to practice in this field. Seaside, for example, is the other end of the spectrum. Since I've been here, my work has been on a smaller scale. In a lot of ways, though, it's just as satisfying because I don't have as many people giving me direction, or second-guessing me, or making changes. So I have more autonomy and an even greater sense of ownership in the work. Of course, there's also a middle ground, where you can find an intensity somewhere between Seaside and New York. Bottom line, I wouldn't discourage anyone from pursuing a career in this field. Just identify what arena you want to play in based on what's required. Now, are there any questions?"

There were quite a few, and Morgan fielded them with humor, polish and savvy. She was disarming in her honesty, admitting her own career gaffes in a selfdeprecating manner that produced a lot of laughs and endeared her to the audience. On a more serious level, she also acknowledged her fundamental mistakes, how she'd gotten so caught up in her job that she'd somehow lost her identity apart from it.

As Grant watched her interact with the young people, as he listened to her confessions and her balanced view of the world she'd once inhabited, he was impressed. He'd wondered, when he'd decided to stay for Morgan's presentation, whether he'd learn anything new about her. And he had. Enough to know that she had changed. Dramatically. And though she hadn't said it in so many words, he suspected that in her own mind she was aiming for that middle ground she'd referred to.

Which meant she wasn't planning to stay in Seaside.

Grant wasn't surprised. But he also experienced an unexpected and profound disappointment that sent his spirits into a tailspin.

"Okay, I'll take one final question," Morgan said as she wrapped things up.

A girl near the front stood. "If you could leave us with one last piece of general advice as we start to think about our careers, what would it be?"

Morgan's gaze flickered to Grant, then just as quickly darted away. When she spoke, her voice was steady, sure and sincere. "It's pretty simple, really. Do what you love. Pursue your dreams. But don't ever let your career come before the things that matter the most. Namely, faith and family." She smiled and gave the room a sweeping glance. "Thank you all for coming tonight."

As the audience enthusiastically applauded, Morgan turned to shake hands with the director of the youth ministry. Grant glanced over at Nancy and Nicki, who had joined a cluster of friends and seemed in no hurry to leave.

"Hey, thanks for filling in tonight," Kit said in his ear.

He turned as she sat beside him. "Have you been here long?"

"I came in about halfway through and took a seat by the door. I was surprised you stayed."

His neck grew warm and he shrugged. "I didn't have anything else to do tonight."

"Hmm." She left her cryptic response open to interpretation and moved on. "Well, I thought Morgan did a great job. And I like how she balanced the good with the bad. She sure has a different attitude than she used to about her work, doesn't she? Remember how stressed she was at Christmas?"

"Yeah. That's not much of a way to live."

"I guess she came to the same conclusion. So, have you thought any more about taking her to the dinner?"

The abrupt change of subject disconcerted him, and his guard went up. "What brought that up?"

"I don't know. I guess it's been on my mind. So have you?"

"I still haven't decided."

"It would be a nice thing to do."

"Yeah."

"Okay, okay, I won't push. I'm going to collect the girls and head home. See you later."

As Kit rounded up the twins and they left, Grant stood. Morgan was still at the front of the room, answering questions from the eager teenagers. Her copper hair glinted in the bright, overhead lights, and her face was animated as she spoke. She wore a classy, sophisticated outfit that he assumed was part of her business wardrobe. The V neck of the fitted jacket revealed the slender column of her throat, where a gold chain glinted against her alabaster skin, and the slim skirt was short enough to call attention to her shapely legs. She was a lovely woman, he acknowledged, who'd had her own struggles these past few months. Her world had been turned upside down, and she was still trying to discover where she belonged. Yet, despite her own problems, she'd thrown herself into the Good Shepherd project and developed a campaign that was reaping amazing results.

As he watched her interact with the young people, he realized that Kit was right. He should take her to the dinner. He owed her that, after all she'd done for the project that was so dear to his heart. The attraction he felt was his problem, after all. She'd done nothing to create it. So he'd just have to deal with it. He couldn't let it get in the way of doing the right thing.

As Morgan turned away from the last student and reached for her notes, she glanced his way. He forced his lips into the semblance of a smile and made his way toward her, stopping a safe distance away. "You were a hit."

She reached up to push the hair back from her face with a fluid gesture indicative of her natural grace. "Thanks. I was surprised to see you."

"The twins needed a lift. Besides, I wanted to talk with you about the Good Shepherd dinner."

Her eyes grew distressed. "Look, Grant, I'm sorry Kit put you in that embarrassing position. Like I said when I dropped off the food after your surgery, don't worry about it. I understand why you'd prefer to go alone—or even skip it, in light of all that's happened."

Once again, he was touched by her consideration. And more certain than ever that Kit's suggestion had been valid. "The timing could be better for me," he admitted. "But Christine would have wanted me to go. She was as committed to the camp as I was. And it doesn't make sense for us to take two cars. I'd be happy to drive you."

When she hesitated, Grant pressed his case. "It's a long drive, Morgan. And you're not that familiar yet with the narrow, winding roads. I'd rather not have to worry about you having car problems or getting lost coming home at such a late hour. You'd be doing me a favor if you'd ride with me."

Put that way, Morgan didn't see how she could refuse him. Nor did she want to, if she was honest with herself. She hadn't been looking forward to the long drive alone. And she enjoyed Grant's company. "All right. But if you change your mind, or decide not to go at all, just let me know."

"I'm committed to being there. We'll work out the details later, but consider it a date."

Even as he said the words, Grant wished he could take them back. This wasn't a date. It was just a friendly gesture. And he didn't want to give Morgan the impression that it was anything more.

As if she'd read his mind, Morgan gave him an understanding smile, though there was a hint of melancholy at the edges. "Hardly. It's just one board member doing a favor for another. And I appreciate it very much."

Her response should have reassured him. But instead of relief, Grant felt a disappointment that scared him.

Because if he looked deep in his heart, he knew that he'd harbored a secret hope that she felt something more for him than friendship— just as he felt something more for her.

Apparently he'd been wrong.

But it was better this way, he told himself. He didn't want to hurt Morgan, and despite the attraction he felt for her, it was too soon even to think about getting involved with anyone else. To do so would dishonor Christine's memory. He should be happy that Morgan viewed their relationship as nothing more than friendship.

But as he said goodbye and turned away, Grant didn't feel happy.

He just felt alone.

Morgan took one last look in the full-length mirror in her bedroom, then gave a satisfied nod. At first she'd worried that she had over-dressed for the black-tie dinner, but even though her dress was long, it was understated and elegant. She should be fine.

As she reached for her small, beaded clutch purse, Morgan glanced at her watch. Grant should be here any minute, she realized, with growing excitement. She knew she was looking forward to this evening with Grant far more than was prudent. As he'd made perfectly clear when he'd issued the invitation, he regarded it as just a convenient, practical gesture. She needed to view it the same way. It was *not* a date.

She repeated that mantra until her pulse quieted. But the minute the doorbell rang, she once more lost control of her heart rate. Get a grip! she admonished herself as she made her way toward the door. Just pretend you're going to another board meeting.

But when she pulled open the door, her casual words of greeting died on her lips. In the elegant tuxedo that emphasized his broad shoulders, Grant definitely did not look like he was on his way to a board meeting. The formal attire gave him a degree of sophistication and worldliness that took her breath away. All she could do was stare.

Grant was glad Morgan didn't speak at once. Because he wasn't sure he would have been able to respond. He'd always known she was an attractive woman. No matter what she wore—from designer jeans and casual sweaters to chic business attire—she always looked perfectly put together. He'd expected the same tonight.

What he hadn't expected was to have the wind knocked out of him by this stunning vision of loveliness and glamour. Morgan wore a simple but elegant black sheath, held up with slim, beaded straps. The same beading continued across the straight bodice, which was cut low enough to suggest, but high enough to be modest, and a simple strand of pearls lay against her silky skin. The beauty of the dress was that it hinted at, rather than revealed, her slender curves. Which, as far as Grant was concerned, made the gown far more alluring than those that were so bare they left little to the imagination.

"Come in," Morgan said at last, stepping aside.

A flash of beads near the floor caught his attention, and his gaze dropped to the slit up the side of the dress that revealed a long length of shapely leg.

Suddenly his collar felt too tight, and he had to restrain himself from reaching up to run a finger around it as he moved past her.

"I guess this is it," she said, trying not to sound out of breath as she closed the door.

"It should be a great evening. Are you ready?"

"All set."

As she reached for her wrap, he took it from her and draped it around her shoulders. Though elegant, the simple satin stole looked none too warm. "I'm not sure this is going to stand up to a Maine night, even if it is May," he cautioned.

"I'll be in the car or the hotel most of the time. I'll be fine," she assured him. Then she grinned. "We women are used to making sacrifices for glamour." She raised the hem of her dress a few inches and wiggled her foot. "See what I mean?"

He glanced down, focusing more on her slender foot than on the flimsy, silver sandal with the narrow straps and high, skinny heel. He cleared his throat and looked back up at her. "I see your point."

She lifted her slender shoulders and smiled. "Nothing but the best for Good Shepherd. But I'll be paying for this tomorrow. There isn't much call for this kind of attire in Seaside, so my feet have gotten pretty used to more comfortable shoes. And they're already protesting."

Grant smiled. "Good Shepherd appreciates your sacrifice. And so do I."

Without giving her time to ponder his remark, he took her arm and guided her toward the door. "Let's get this show on the road."

With his hand under her elbow, Morgan picked her way across the gravel drive in front of Aunt Jo's cottage. In her formal attire, she needed some assistance getting up to the running board, and his hands were strong and sure on her waist as he boosted her up.

"Thanks." Her voice was a bit unsteady as she swung her legs inside.

"My pleasure," he said, the look in his eyes making her breath catch in her throat.

The ride to Portland passed quickly. Too quickly for Morgan. Grant kept their banter light, but there was no denying the connection between them. It made her nerve endings tingle in a delicious way, unlike anything she'd ever experienced with another man. She suspected Grant was as conscious of it as she was, but unlike her, he seemed to have a firm grip on his emotions. From the minute he'd appeared at her door tonight, she'd forgotten all of the many reasons why she shouldn't even consider a relationship with this man. At least one of them was being sensible.

Once they arrived at the benefit, Grant was kept busy. As the chairman, he was expected to greet all of the important guests during the cocktail hour. That was fine with Morgan; she needed some time apart from him to try and regain some perspective. Nevertheless, she found her gaze wandering to him again and again as she nibbled on hors d'oeuvres, sipped sparkling water and chatted with Kit and Bill.

"Isn't this place something?" Kit said, her eyes flashing with excitement as she snagged a crab rangoon from the tray of a passing waiter, then peeked into the adjacent hotel ballroom.

Morgan looked over her shoulder, admiring the lovely setting. The tables were draped with crisp, white linen, and the mauve chair covers were held in place by gauzy silver bows on the back. Enormous crystal chandeliers hung overhead, but they'd been dimmed to allow the long tapers in the dramatic floral centerpieces on each table to add a warm glow to the room. A string quartet played in the anteroom, where the drinks were being served, adding to the elegant ambiance.

"I bet you've been to a lot of events like this," Kit said, turning to Morgan.

"A few. But this one is special."

"True. And it wouldn't have happened without you."

Morgan made a dismissive gesture. "A lot of people worked hard to make this evening a success."

"Well, I know Grant is pleased. Where is he, by the way?"

"You've got me. He was pulled away seconds after we stepped in the door. I haven't seen him since," Morgan told her.

Kit made a face. "I wish he could just relax and enjoy the evening. But at least you two will be having dinner at the same table, right?"

"That's the plan."

"Good." At the sound of a gong, Kit took Bill's arm. "Time to eat."

"You haven't stopped eating since you arrived," he teased her.

She gave him a playful punch in the arm. "Hey, I don't get to go to many of these fancy doings. Cut me some slack. Besides, I noticed you had your share of shrimp cocktails."

"Guilty as charged," he admitted with a chuckle.

"We'll see you later, Morgan," Kit promised as they headed off to find their table.

"Okay. Have fun," she called after them. As Morgan dug in her purse to find the card with her table number on it, she felt a hand in the small of her back and looked up to find Grant smiling down at her.

"Sorry I got waylaid."

Her heart tripped into double time and she had to use every ounce of her willpower to keep herself from leaning back into his hand. "No problem. Kit and Bill kept me company. And we sampled all the hors d'oeuvres."

"Were they good?"

She looked at him in surprise. "Didn't you try any?"

"I didn't have a chance," he said with regret. "But I plan to make up for it at dinner."

With a gentle pressure on her back, he guided her into the dining room and toward their table.

But again, they had little time to themselves. The woman seated on Grant's right—a major donor to the camp—kept him occupied during most of the dinner, leaving Morgan to make conversation with an elderly gentleman on her left. After dinner, the big-name entertainment drew everyone's attention, and then the master of ceremonies took over.

As the winners of the silent auction were announced, Morgan leaned back in her chair and eased her feet out of her shoes. Her toes might be protesting, but as she surveyed the packed ballroom, a warm glow of satisfaction spread through her. The dinner had been a resounding success. Every table had been sold, guests had made generous bids in the silent auction and contributions had poured in. The camp was in its best financial position ever, and Morgan's suggested advisory board of prominent people was in place to spearhead future fund-raising efforts. Aunt Jo would be pleased, Morgan thought with a smile.

"A penny for your thoughts."

She turned to Grant, her smile still in place. "I don't think we're in the penny league tonight."

"True," he agreed. "I saw some of the bids for that trip to Cancun. They were way out of *my* league, that's for sure. So what do I have to offer to find out what prompted that smile?"

"No charge. I was just thinking how happy Aunt Jo would be with the way things turned out for Good Shepherd."

"She'd be thrilled," he concurred.

"I wish she could see this."

"I like to think she's here in spirit. And I expect she's very proud of you. You did a fabulous job, and I…"

"Grant! I've been trying to make my way over here all evening. How are you?"

Startled, Grant glanced up, then rose. "What are you doing here?"

The woman laughed. "Is that any way to greet your mother? Don't I get a hug or anything?"

With obvious reluctance, Grant leaned forward, gave the woman a brief embrace, then backed off. "So why *are* you here?" he repeated.

"Alan Davidson, our president, is an alumni of Good Shepherd. Can you believe it? Anyway, he bought a table. I was supposed to be out of the country, but the trip fell through at the last minute and they still had a seat available. So here I am. It's a wonderful event."

"Thanks to Morgan." Grant reached for her hand and drew Morgan to her feet. "Mom, I'd like you to meet Morgan Williams. She's serving as an advisory member of the Good Shepherd board and developed this event. Morgan, this is my mother, Ellen Kincaid."

Morgan held out her hand, and the other woman took it in a firm clasp. Up close, she looked older than Morgan remembered from the funeral, but she'd only seen her from a distance on that occasion. Nevertheless, Grant's mother had style. Her clingy claret-colored gown showed off her excellent figure, and Morgan's practiced eye recognized the touch of a well-known designer in the cut.

"My pleasure," Ellen said with a smile. "And congratulations on a stellar event."

"A lot of people contributed to the effort," Morgan replied.

"Yes, I recognized quite a few of the names on the advisory board in the program. And the guests are a veritable who's who of movers and shakers in Boston. I ran into a number of our clients tonight, and even managed to get an appointment with someone we've been trying to do business with for years."

"It sounds as though it's been a profitable evening for you," Grant said dryly.

"It has. I'm so glad I came!" his mother gushed, oblivious to the irony in his tone. "Oh, look! Is that John Patton over there? I'm sure it is. I need to say hello. He's one of our major clients."

"Kit's here somewhere, too," Grant told her.

"Oh? I'll have to try and find her." His mother's tone was vague as she attempted to keep the man she'd spotted in sight. At last, with obvious effort, she pulled her attention back to the two people standing before her. "It was a pleasure meeting you, Morgan."

"Likewise."

"Take care, Grant."

"You, too."

They watched her close in on her quarry, then Grant looked at Morgan and shook his head as they sat down again. "Typical Mom. Work is always top of mind."

Morgan stared after the woman, but she'd disappeared into the crowd. "You know, I see myself in her," she admitted. "And it's not a pretty picture."

"I don't see you that way anymore."

A warm glow spread through Morgan as she turned back to Grant. "I'm glad. Because I think I've seen the light. It's too bad your mom doesn't."

He played with his water glass, his eyes thoughtful. "I doubt she ever will. Mom is just…Mom. She was never happy in Maine. Dad and Kit accepted that a long time ago. But I was just angry. For a very long time."

"I can understand that. I can't even imagine how I'd have felt if my mom had left us to pursue a career in another city."

"Anger doesn't help anyone, though." His expression was pensive as he stared into the crowd. "Dad and Kit and Uncle Pete have been telling me that for years. And you know what I just realized? The last couple of times I've seen Mom—tonight, and at the funeral—the anger was gone. It's like I've finally accepted that this is how she is and just let the anger go. It wasn't even a conscious decision."

"However you arrived there, I'm sure it's a healthier place to be."

"Kit would no doubt agree with you," he said with a smile. "And I have to admit it's a freeing feeling. Like a heavy load had been lifted from my shoulders. I'm not sure why it took me so long to get here."

"Things happen when they're supposed to happen. Maybe you weren't ready to let the anger go until recently."

"Yeah. Letting go can be tough."

From the subtle shift in his tone, she had the distinct feeling that he wasn't talking about anger anymore.

"And now, to start off the dancing portion of the evening, I'll call upon the chairman of the board, Grant Kincaid."

It took a second for the voice of the emcee to register, and when it did, Grant looked startled. "I didn't know about this," he muttered as the room erupted into applause.

Morgan leaned closer. "Don't you dance?"

"I haven't been on a dance floor in years."

On impulse, Morgan reached for his hand and urged him to his feet. "Well, I'm a bit rusty myself. But maybe we can muddle through together." Then she leaned closer still. "I think it's expected. Can your knee handle this?"

"Yeah." But he wasn't so sure about his heart.

When he hesitated, Morgan faltered, regretting her spontaneous action. "Would you rather dance with Kit?" she offered.

He shook his head as a smile tugged at the corners of his mouth. "Don't ever tell her I said this, but she has two left feet."

"You may say the same about me by the time we're finished," Morgan warned him with a chuckle.

He twined his fingers with hers and shook his head. "Somehow I doubt that."

As he led her to the dance floor, then turned to pull her into his arms, the orchestra struck up the classic melody of "Unforgettable."

And as they began to sway to the rhythm, Morgan had only one word for the music, the moment, and the man: perfect.

Without a doubt, the event was unforgettable. It had been everything they'd hoped for. According to the tally at the April board meeting, the dinner alone had netted close to a quarter of a million dollars, and the auction was expected to bring in another sizeable chunk of money.

But this interlude in Grant's arms was also unforgettable. With his hand resting on the small of her back, urging her closer to him, Morgan felt as though she was in heaven. She could smell the heady scent of his aftershave, and with a contented sigh, she moved closer and tucked her head into his shoulder.

The effect of their closeness also had a powerful impact on Grant. Morgan felt so good in his arms—and so right. He rested his cheek against her silky hair and inhaled, relishing the appealing fragrance, as she moved with an easy grace to the lovely strains of the timeless melody. Over the past several months, he'd learned that Morgan was an intriguing study in contrasts. She was strong, yet vulnerable. Beautiful, but not conceited. Talented, yet modest.

She was truly unforgettable.

When the music drew to a close, Grant stepped back and looked down at her luminous face. And for one brief, glorious instant before he managed to shutter his eyes, the sounds of the room faded and their hearts touched.

And as they turned away to take their seats, he knew one thing with absolute certainty.

The dance had ended.

But something else had begun.

Chapter Twelve

Grant reached up to loosen his tie and glanced over at Morgan, who was asleep in his truck. The dinner had run far later then either of them had expected, and though she'd tried to stay awake during the drive home, her eyelids had finally drifted closed. She'd been out for the past forty-five minutes. So Grant had had time to think about several things.

Like his feelings about his mother. Or, more accurately, his lack of feelings. In the past, the anger he'd nursed all these years had bubbled up every time he was in her presence. Tonight, there had been no anger. Nor had there been any at the funeral. While he might not agree with what she had done twenty-five years ago, he had finally accepted that it was history. And he'd gone on with his life. She was now just someone who popped in and out of his world every now and then. If anything, he felt sorry for her. Because of the path she had chosen, she'd missed out on a lot of the things that really mattered.

As for the dinner, it had been successful beyond his wildest hopes, leaving the camp financially secure for the foreseeable future. And for that he owed Jo a deep debt of gratitude. Without the stipulation in her will that had mandated Morgan's involvement, he wasn't sure that Good Shepherd would have survived even another season. Now, and for a long time to come, it would be able to continue the work that had helped so many young people.

But mostly Grant thought about Morgan. It wasn't just her loveliness that attracted him. Over the past few months, he'd come to recognize her deeper beauty. She was an intelligent, kind, caring woman who, once committed to a cause or a project, gave her all, holding nothing back. She was also a survivor, a woman who was willing to admit her mistakes, learn from them, and move on. She'd demonstrated that resiliency during these past few months.

But the trauma had taken its toll.

Once more, he turned his head towards her. In repose, her face was relaxed, the tension hidden. But the faint lines at the corners of her eyes, which hadn't been there in December, and the too-prominent bone structure of her face, which reminded him that she'd lost weight, spoke of stress and uncertainty and strain. Morgan's life was still on hold, and major decisions about her future lay ahead. She lived with that unsettling pressure and anxiety every day.

Grant knew that one day soon, someone in the corporate world would recognize Morgan's talents and try to lure her back into the rat race she'd been forced to leave. Based on her comments at the youth meeting, he didn't think that kind of life appealed to her anymore. But he also knew that with the right offer, she could be tempted to return to her former high-stakes, fast-paced world. Unless she had a reason to stay in Seaside. A compelling reason.

A reason that he wasn't yet ready to offer.

Despite Bill's encouragement, and despite that incredible moment on the dance floor when his heart had connected with Morgan's, it just felt too soon.

Grant turned into the driveway of Serenity Point, sure that the jostling of the truck on the uneven lane and the crunch of gravel beneath the tires would awaken Morgan. But she continued to sleep soundly, even as he pulled to a stop and turned off the engine. The opportunity to drink in her beauty unobserved was so rare that he indulged himself. He noted how the moonlight turned her skin luminous, admired the graceful sweep of her lashes against her cheeks, marveled at the delicate line of her jaw, let his gaze linger on her soft lips. And in spite of his resolve to keep his distance, the urge to gather her close in his arms was compelling.

Morgan opened her eyes just then, and whatever she saw in his made her own grow wide. As surprise softened to welcome, Grant's mouth went dry.

With superhuman effort, he turned away and fumbled for the handle of his door. "Sit tight. I'll come around," he mumbled.

Taking his time, Grant circled the truck, drawing deep breaths of the chilly air, trying to clear his head—and trying to suppress the guilt that gnawed at him. Would Christine be hurt to know that he had such strong feelings for someone else so soon, he wondered? Or would she understand his loneliness, perhaps even encourage him to find a new love?

Grant didn't know the answers to those questions. And Christine's voice was silent. All he knew was that right now, despite a powerful yearning to touch the vibrant, desirable woman he'd spent the evening with, this didn't feel right. No matter how much he wanted it. So he needed to say good-night and go home.

Resolving to make a fast exit, Grant reached up and opened Morgan's door. In the dim overhead light, her face was in shadows—and unreadable. In silence, she swung her legs to the running board and made a move to stand. But her elegant, high-heeled sandals hadn't been designed for stability on a ridged surface. She lost her footing, and his arms shot out to steady her. The next thing he knew, her hands were on his shoulders, and without even stopping to think, he reached for her waist and swung her to the ground.

And he didn't let her go.

It had been a long time since Grant had held a woman in his arms. Almost three years. Three endless, lonely years. Three years of going to bed alone and waking up alone. While his family had done their best to fill the void, nothing could replace the joys offered by a wonderful, fulfilling marriage. And nothing made up for the tender touch of someone with whom you were in love.

Grant didn't think he was in love with Morgan. He couldn't be. It was too soon. But the temptation to kiss her was strong. And the look in her wide, appealing eyes told him she was willing.

With an unsteady hand, he touched her face—and heard her sharp intake of breath. The moonlight shimmering on her face gave her an ethereal beauty that took his own breath away. Gently, he cupped her face with his hands, stroking her cheeks with his thumbs, delaying the inevitable as long as possible as he savored the intense sweetness of this moment. But at last, with a tenderness bordering on reverence, he lowered his lips to hers.

Grant wasn't sure how long the kiss lasted. When he finally pulled back—with reluctance—he kept his arms looped around her waist as he searched her face, noting that the dazed look in her eyes mirrored his own feelings.

In his heart, Grant knew that he shouldn't have let things go so far tonight. And he didn't want to create expectations he wasn't prepared to follow up on. That would only hurt Morgan. And she didn't need any more stress in her life.

"Morgan, I…I'm sorry," he whispered.

Her eyes registered confusion, then hurt. With a sudden sharp movement, she stepped back, forcing him to drop his arms.

"Thanks for…for the ride," she whispered. And without another word she turned and almost ran to the cottage. Before he could react, she fumbled for her key, inserted it in the lock and slipped inside, shutting the door behind her with a decisive click.

A muscle in Grant's jaw twitched, and he closed his eyes, balling his hands into fists. He hadn't wanted to hurt Morgan. Yet he'd done exactly that. All because he'd given in to temptation. And now the damage was done.

With a heavy heart, he turned toward his truck, glancing once more at the closed door of the cottage before he pulled out of the drive. He needed to make amends in some way. But he didn't know how.

On the other side of the door, Morgan stood trembling, eyes closed, struggling to corral her chaotic emotions. When the crunch of gravel signaled Grant's departure, she fought back a sob. She hadn't expected him to kiss her tonight. She'd understood that propriety, and a wish to honor Christine's memory, were serious obstacles to any relationship for him right now. So his kiss had been a surprise. One that had left her breathless. And hopeful.

Until his parting comment.

Grant was sorry he'd kissed her.

Which meant he wasn't in the market for romance now. And maybe never would be. He'd simply succumbed to a moment of weakness in the moonlight. And it wasn't going to happen again. That message had been clear.

Morgan drew a shaky breath. Why, when a man who appealed to her crossed her path, did his heart have to belong to another? And why did his lifestyle have to be so at odds with hers? Grant had made no secret of the fact that Maine was his home—and always would be. She had no idea where she might end up. But she didn't think these rocky shores were her final destination. Even if he wanted her to stay. Even if he could put the past aside and move on. Two possibilities which seemed as remote as the distant stars she sometimes pondered in the midnight sky of rural Maine.

With a heavy heart, Morgan slipped out of her evening gown, marking the official end of the magical evening. And when she climbed into bed and scrunched her pillow under her head, her heart heavy and her soul weary, she did something she hadn't done since her father died.

She cried herself to sleep.

Morgan dialed the phone, then lowered herself into a chair on Aunt Jo's deck and raised her face to the warm May sun as she waited for Clare to answer so they could have their weekly chat.

When her sister's voice came over the line, Morgan smiled. "You sound happy."

"It's a beautiful day here," Clare replied. "How is it there?"

"Gorgeous. I'm enjoying the view of the sea as we speak."

"Sounds great! How's the job search going?"

"Nothing yet. But I'm keeping busy with local work."

"Have you given any thought to staying?"

"A little." Morgan focused her eyes on the distant lighthouse. "It's kind of strange, Clare. When I lost my job in January, I thought my life was over. Instead, I ended up finding my life. The work I'm doing now is less stressful, and I have time for other things. Better yet, I got my priorities straightened out. I'll never sacrifice my family or my faith again in pursuit of worldly success."

"Then I'd say your time in Maine has been very worthwhile, no matter where you go from there."

"I agree."

"So have you and Grant worked out the disposition of the cottage?"

"No." She hadn't seen Grant since the fund-raiser ten days before. "We haven't even talked about it yet. But the six months is up at the end of the month, so we're going to need to discuss it soon. What are your plans after your nanny gig is over?"

"I'm not sure."

"A.J. told me the same thing. I guess we're all in the same boat. Would you consider staying in North Carolina?"

There was a telling moment of silence. "If the right offer came along," Clare replied.

That was the closest Clare had come to admitting that she'd fallen in love with her young charge's father. And it gave Morgan the opening she needed to discuss her own situation. "I kind of feel the same way," Morgan admitted.

For years Morgan hadn't shared much of her personal life with her sisters, and she knew Clare didn't want to appear nosy. So when Clare broached the question Morgan was waiting for, her voice was cautious. "Have you by any chance fallen in love with Grant?"

"As a matter of fact...yes."

"But Morgan—that's wonderful!"

"It's also complicated."

"How?"

"For one thing, a commitment to him would

be a lifetime commitment to Seaside. He's made it very clear that this is his home and it always will be."

"Is that so bad?"

"Believe it or not, no. I like it here. And I can still work in my field. It's just not the life I envisioned."

"Maybe it's a better one."

"True. But that's not the major hurdle. Grant was very much in love with his wife. I think his heart still belongs to her. And I'm afraid maybe it always will."

"'Always' is a long time, Morgan. He's been through a rough three years, from everything you've told me. And she's only been gone a few weeks. He may just need some time."

"Yeah. I keep telling myself that. But patience has never been my strong suit."

"Well, I don't think it would be wise to rush this situation. Why not put it in the Lord's hands? And pray. That always helps."

"Trust me, I've been doing that."

"Then He'll answer. In His own time."

In her heart, Morgan believed that.

She just wished He'd hurry up.

Grant sat back on his heels, bone weary, and ran a hand down his face. The task he'd set for himself today had drained him. But it had been time. For all of the years Christine had been in a coma, he'd left her clothing and personal items untouched in the bedroom, as if awaiting her return. Even though she'd been gone for more than four months now, he hadn't found the courage to take this last step. There was such finality about disposing of the things that had belonged to someone you loved. But since today was their anniversary, thoughts of her were on his mind, anyway. And somehow it had seemed an appropriate time to touch once more the things that had been part of her. To remember. To grieve one last time. And finally to close the door on the past.

He surveyed the boxes scattered around the room and on the bed. Most were full. He'd already been through the closet, and he was now down to the last drawer. Soon he would be finished, though that thought gave him little comfort.

As he'd gone through her clothing, folding each item with care before placing it in the box for charity, he'd wished she could return, for just a moment, to tell him in her gentle voice that it was time for him to bring to a close the chapter of his life they'd shared and to start a new one. But her voice was as silent as it had been for three long years. So he would have to listen to his heart and make the decision for himself, trusting that she would understand and approve.

The last drawer was filled with sweaters and he removed them one by one, until only a pink angora sweater remained—one of her favorites, he recalled with a pang. He reached for it with an aching heart, and as he withdrew the soft, wool garment, Christine's sweet fragrance enveloped him. He lifted the sweater to his face and inhaled deeply as a rush of memories spilled over him, constricting his throat with emotion as he struggled to contain the hot tears that stung the back of his eyes. For several seconds he held it to his face. Then he gently laid it in the box and closed the lid.

With a sense of finality, Grant rose, taped the lid shut and carried all of the boxes to the garage. The charity he'd selected would pick them up tomorrow.

Feeling lonelier than he had in a long time, Grant returned to the house, poured himself a cup of coffee, and made his way out to the gazebo in the backyard. He'd built it for Christine on their first anniversary, and it had been one of her favorite spots. Nestled in fir trees, it was a perfect place for contemplation, or reading, or praying…or saying goodbye.

Grant had spent little time there since Christine's death. It reminded him too much of her—and of all he'd lost. But today he found some comfort sitting in the Adirondack chair she had loved and looking at the view of the sun-filtered woods that she'd always enjoyed. She'd often told him that whenever she needed to think a problem through, she'd come out here. And more often than not, by the time she returned to the house, she had her answer.

Grant could use some answers about now, he thought with a sigh. He still loved Christine. He always would. But he'd also fallen in love with Morgan. How could that be?

As he settled back in his chair, his shoulders drooping, the corner of a magazine peeking out of the drawer in the small side table beside him caught his eye. Curious, he pulled it out, marveling that it had survived three Maine winters. Other than brittle pages, it bore no sign of age or damage. Christine must have left it here, he realized.

The Christian magazine was turned back to an article titled, "Make Today Count" And Christine had highlighted several key sentences.

We must always remember that each day from God is a gift. The past is gone, and regret is futile. Tomorrow is not promised to us, so all of our plans may be for naught. But we have today. Let us resolve to live fully, love much and trust in the Lord.

Setting the magazine aside, Grant stood and wrapped his hands around his coffee mug, his expression pensive. The message in the article must have resonated with Christine. And now, in an odd twist of fate, she'd passed it on to him when he needed it most.

A sudden gust of wind whipped past, and a flutter of yellow caught his attention. Looking down, he saw a single, late-blooming daffodil swaying in the breeze. Daffodils had been Christine's favorite flower, he recalled with a pang. She'd always thought of them as brave and hopeful, because they were among the first flowers to seek the sun after the long, dark days of winter. She'd surrounded the gazebo with them, and awaited their appearance each spring with eager anticipation. Why this one had bloomed so late, he didn't know. But somehow it seemed significant.

Grant wasn't a superstitious person, or someone inclined to believe in signs from above. But finding both the magazine and the daffodil seemed too providential to be mere coincidence.

And with sudden clarity, the direction and guidance that had so long eluded him was revealed.

It was time to move on.

Loving someone else would never diminish what he and Christine had found, Grant realized, his insight sharp and sure. That would always be theirs alone. But there was room in his heart for someone new. Someone who would fill his todays with love and laughter. And his tomorrows, as well, with God's blessing. But he was only going to count on today.

And he didn't intend to waste one more of those.

Morgan stared at the message in her e-mail.

She was being asked to interview for a job. Not just any job. A great job. With a major agency. In New York City.

It was the kind of job she'd always dreamed of having.

Morgan read the message again. There was a time when such an opportunity would have thrilled her. But after all that had happened since January, she wasn't that excited. Or even that interested. In fact, the only emotion she felt was conflict. Because if she pursued this opportunity, and it led to an offer, she'd have to choose between a once-in-a-lifetime job and her life in Seaside, which she had come to love—along with a very special, once-in-a-lifetime man.

And therein lay the crux of the problem. Even though she and Grant were just friends, in her heart she felt that, given time, they could be more. But what if she was wrong? What if she passed up this opportunity and nothing ever developed with Grant? Would she want to stay in Seaside alone?

Morgan didn't know the answer to those questions.

But it was time to think long and hard about them before she passed up the opportunity that now dangled before her.

Grant pulled to a stop in front of Serenity Point, besieged by sudden doubts as he fingered the small box that was tucked into the pocket of his jeans. For most of the six months they'd known each other, he and Morgan had been mere friends. But the kiss had changed things. For him, anyway, and he hoped for her, too. Considering his abrupt departure the night of the benefit though, and the hurt in her eyes when he'd said he was sorry, maybe she'd just tell him to get lost.

Or maybe not.

In any case, it was time to find out.

Steeling his resolve, Grant climbed out of his truck and strode toward the door. When his first knock went unanswered, he tried again. Her sporty little car was parked beside the cottage, so he knew she was home. Maybe she was on the deck. Or had gone for a walk. It was a beautiful day.

He checked the deck, but it was empty. Frustrated, he lifted a hand to shade his eyes and looked out at the whitecap-dotted sea. Although this view often calmed him, today it didn't work its typical magic. He doubted anything could quiet the rapid thump of his heart. As he scanned the shore, a glint of copper at the point of Jo's land caught his eye, and he drew in a sharp breath. Morgan was there. On the secluded bench Jo had loved.

Now that the moment was upon him, Grant was scared. The temptation to turn and run away was strong. But he couldn't run away from his feelings. And it was time to share them. If he was wrong, if Morgan didn't return his love, he'd have to deal with it sooner or later. There was no reason to delay the inevitable.

She didn't hear him until he was almost upon her, and when she turned her eyes widened in surprise.

"Hi," he said, forcing his stiff lips into the semblance of a smile. "May I?" He inclined his head toward the bench.

"Of course." She scooted over to make room for him.

He sat beside her, wishing the distant lighthouse would provide him with the same guidance it had given to so many storm-tossed ships. He was in uncharted territory here, and was afraid he was about to flounder. *Please be with me, Lord,* he pleaded. *Help me find the right words.*

Gathering up his courage, he turned to her. "I've missed you since the night of the benefit."

She gave him a cautious look, and he noted the lines of tension and strain around her mouth and eyes.

"Is everything okay?" he asked, when she didn't respond.

"I guess you could say that. I've been asked to interview for a job in New York."

It was Grant's worst nightmare, and his stomach clenched in a painful knot. In the back of his mind he'd always expected this day to come, had known that sooner or later someone would recognize Morgan's talent and make her a tempting offer. But why did it have to be now? When he'd decided to take Bill's advice and give her a reason to stay, make an offer of his own? How could he compete with a glitzy New York job? And, did he even want to? What if she picked him, but later resented all she'd given up to stay in a tiny backwater town like Seaside? He'd been through that once with his mother. He didn't want to go there again.

He managed to speak in a calm, controlled voice that gave no hint of his inner turmoil. "Are you going to do the interview?"

"Do you think I should?" she countered, searching his face.

He swallowed hard. "That's your decision."

It wasn't the answer she wanted. Disappointed, she looked back at the sea. If Grant had feelings for her, he wasn't revealing them. And maybe he never would. As she'd told Clare, Grant's love for Christine had been deep and true. There might not be room in his heart for another woman. Now. Or ever.

Morgan still wasn't sure she wanted to go back to big-city life. She seemed to have moved past whatever fascination she'd had with the world of high-stakes business meetings, power lunches and ego trips. At the same time, she supposed she owed it to herself to at least explore what she knew was the opportunity of a lifetime. Especially since she didn't have any better offers.

"I guess I'll talk to them," she told Grant.

He nodded, even as his heart began to break. "That probably makes sense."

Calling on every bit of acting ability she possessed, Morgan summoned up the semblance of a smile. "So what brought you out here on this beautiful day?"

"Just paying a neighborly visit. But I need to get going. I still have to make a delivery this afternoon." He rose and jammed his hands in his pockets, his fingers tightening around the small box.

"I'll walk you to your truck."

"No!" His hand shot to her shoulder to restrain her, and she sank back on the bench with a startled look. "I don't want to take you away from this beautiful view," he amended, softening his tone. And then, though the words almost choked him, he added, "Good luck with the job interview."

There was a wistful, melancholy look in her eyes when she replied. "Thanks."

He lifted a hand in response, then turned and

strode away. And with each step he took away from her, his heart grew heavier. Maybe he should have told her how he felt, asked her to forget about the job in New York and stay. He almost had. But something had held him back. Something he hadn't been able to define until now.

Fear.

Fear that she'd reject him.

Fear that she'd accept, and later come to resent him for holding her back.

Both possibilities scared him to death.

And he wasn't sure how to overcome that.

For three long years, even on his darkest days, Grant had found comfort in God's abiding presence. And so he once again turned to Him for consolation and direction.

Lord, I'm in a quandary, he prayed. *I can't imagine letting Morgan walk away, but I don't want her to end up unhappy because of me. Please guide me. Help me to understand Your will, and give me the courage to follow it.*

Grant was open to God's voice. But in his heart, he hoped that the Lord would help him find a way to convince Morgan to stay, willingly and with no regrets.

Because he didn't know if he could find the courage to go on without her.

Chapter Thirteen

The job was hers.

Morgan leaned back in her seat and closed her eyes, the steady, even drone of the airplane providing a contrasting backdrop for her turbulent emotions.

It had been an invigorating day. She'd lunched with the vice president of the firm, then spent the afternoon talking with a number of senior-level people. Without missing a beat, she'd slipped back into the fast-paced, rapid-fire mentality of the advertising world, and her adrenaline had been running high all day. She knew she'd aced the interviews, but even so, she'd been taken aback when an offer had been made even before she'd left.

It had been a heady experience, one that left her feeling good—and validated. Hours later, she was still elated and excited. The job was everything she'd ever dreamed of, offering all the things that had once been so important to her—a generous salary, hefty bonus, fabulous perks and far more power and prestige than she'd enjoyed in her previous position.

A year ago, she would have signed on the dotted line with no hesitation.

But now her euphoria was tempered by something she hadn't had even six months before—perspective. She knew the job would entail more stress, less personal time, sixty-hour weeks. She'd be back in the fast lane and expected to put her work first, with everything else in her life relegated to a distant second place. Those sacrifices would be the trade-off for the power, prestige and perks.

Morgan had lived that life for a long time. And she wasn't sure she wanted to go back. So she'd asked for a few days to think over the offer.

She opened her eyes, enjoying the view of the billowing clouds as the plane began its descent to Portland. After her hectic day in noisy, crowded New York City, she was looking forward to going home, she realized, as the tension in her shoulders began to ease.

And as she buckled her seatbelt, she realized

something else. Something startling about her choice of words.

Seaside had, indeed, become home.

And, with or without Grant, she didn't want to leave.

Her hands stilled on the buckle as she grappled with that insight. It had been a long time since she'd felt at home anywhere. But she did in Seaside. Because she had found there the same things that had drawn Aunt Jo back year after year—serenity, peace of mind and perspective. And Morgan didn't want to give them up. She loved the cottage. She enjoyed the work she was doing, which would give her a comfortable, if not luxurious, lifestyle. But she didn't need the luxury items she'd once thought essential. She preferred the simpler life of rural Maine.

The plane touched down, and as Morgan gathered up her briefcase and jacket, she was filled with a deep sense of contentment and peace of mind, as well as a cathartic feeling of freedom. For she now knew, deep in her heart and with absolute certainty, that she no longer needed the trappings of the high-stakes world she had once held in such high esteem. Her old life no longer had the power to attract her. It had lost its appeal. She'd found something better.

It was time to go home, to where she belonged.

"When does Morgan get back?"

Grant took a sip of his coffee as he watched Kit, who was busy at the stove. "Later tonight. Thanks again for inviting me to dinner."

"You're always welcome. You know that. So, are you going to call her?"

So much for trying to distract his one-track-mind sister. "Not tonight. She didn't expect to get home until after eleven."

"Do you think they'll offer her the job?"

"Probably."

Kit turned from the stove, a frown on her face. "Yeah. I think so, too."

"I thought of asking her to stay." He stared into his coffee, his voice subdued.

"And...?"

"She might not be happy here long-term. I don't want to tie her to Seaside if she has bigger ambitions."

Kit tossed him a shrewd look. "Are we talking about Morgan or Mom?"

"There are similarities."

"Only on a superficial level. Morgan's already experienced the fast lane. I think she's ready to trade it for a more reasonable life. Which she could have here in Seaside. With you."

"I just don't want to hold her back."

"Why don't you trust her to make that decision for herself? If she wants to take the job, she'll take it. But there's nothing wrong with giving her an incentive to stay here. And love is a pretty good one."

"I'm not sure it's good enough."

Kit reached over and laid her hand over his. "Why don't you let her decide?"

When he didn't respond, Kit cut right to the chase. "Don't let fear hold you back, Grant." At his startled look, she gave him an impish smile. "You ought to know by now that I have amazing powers of perception. Although it doesn't take a genius to figure out what's going on here. And I understand why you're afraid. But I'd hate for you to miss out on your chance for happiness because of fear. Why not put it in God's hands?"

The twins came in then, laughing and chattering, and Kit transferred her attention to them after giving Grant's hand one final, encouraging squeeze.

As usual, his sister's insight was right on target. Fear *was* holding him back. He'd identified it himself, earlier.

But all at once he realized that there was something else that scared him even more than rejection or potential down-the-road resentment.

Namely, spending the rest of his life without Morgan.

So, he was left with only one course of action.

And he resolved to take it first thing tomorrow, after what he knew would be a long, sleepless night.

Morgan read the letter a second time, changed a couple of words, then, with a sense of finality, sent it to the printer. The decision was made.

She poured herself a cup of coffee and wandered out to the deck, lifting her face to the morning sun as she basked in its warmth. If she was in Boston or New York right now, she'd be fighting the commuter crowds and listening to honking horns and the other sounds of big-city life. As it was, her solitude was broken only by an occasional chipmunk or seagull. And except for the sound of the waves lapping at the shore and the whisper of wind in the pine trees, the stillness was absolute. She couldn't imagine any place she'd rather be, she thought with contentment.

"Good morning."

Morgan turned in surprise at the sound of Grant's voice, unable to stop the warm rush of pleasure triggered by his mere presence. "Hi."

"When you didn't answer the door, I figured you'd be here or on the bench. So how did it go yesterday?" He came up beside her and propped his hip against the railing, folding his arms across his chest.

"Pretty well, I guess. They offered me the job."

He fought against the panic that swept over him. "I'm happy they recognized your talent. And I'm not surprised by the offer. I knew one of these days someone would realize what an asset you'd be and try to lure you back to the big city."

"I have to admit, it was great for my ego," she acknowledged with a grin.

Grant shoved his hand into the pocket of his jeans and fingered the small box, praying for the courage to follow his heart. "You didn't need a job offer to validate your worth, Morgan."

"I know. But it still felt good."

"I'm sure it did." He cleared his throat and

drew a steadying breath. "And speaking of jobs, I'd like to make a counter offer."

"A counter offer?" she repeated, puzzled.

"Well, it's not a job, exactly. More like a partnership."

Morgan's heart stopped, then raced on. Don't jump to any conclusions, she admonished herself. He might be talking about Serenity Point.

"What did you have in mind?" Her voice cautious, she gripped her mug with both hands to keep it steady.

"Let's go down to Aunt Jo's bench and talk about it there, okay?"

Unable to find her voice, she gave a muted nod. When she placed her mug on the railing, Grant reached for her hand, lacing his fingers with hers. With growing excitement, she let him lead her off the deck and down the soft, pine-needle-strewn path to the bench. Once there he sat, tugging her down beside him. But he didn't relinquish her hand. And when he looked at her, what she saw in his eyes took Morgan's breath away. Gone were the walls. Gone was the caution. She had a clear view right into his heart. And what she saw was unmistakable.

Love.

In all its absolute, complete, unrestrained glory.

When Grant began to speak, it took every ounce of Morgan's willpower to focus on his words rather than his eyes.

"I hope this doesn't come as too much of a shock to you, Morgan, because I know up until now we've just been friends. And maybe not even that, at the beginning," he admitted, one corner of his mouth quirking into a wry grin. "But the fact is, over these past few months I've learned a thing or two. About you. And about myself."

As he spoke he began to stroke the back of her hand gently with his thumb. "First, about you. When we met, I wrote you off as a gung-ho, ambitious career woman whose priorities were way out of whack. To be honest, you reminded me a lot of my mother. And that turned me off. But when you lost your job and came up here, I started to see another side of you. I was impressed by your total commitment to the Good Shepherd project, even though it had been forced on you. I admired the way you dealt with a world that was disintegrating around you. I watched as you found your way back to God, and as you re-evaluated and re-established your priorities. I respected your honesty and your good humor and your talent. I recognized your kindness and intelligence. I appreciated your physical beauty from the beginning, of course. But as I got to know you, I realized that your beauty went a lot deeper. That beneath all the big-city glamour and sophistication, you had a tender and caring heart."

In a gesture both tentative and sure, Grant reached over and laid a gentle hand against her cheek. When he spoke again, his voice had deepened. "The fact is, somewhere along the way I fell in love with you, Morgan. I didn't want to. And I felt enormous guilt about it because of Christine. But I couldn't deny my feelings, even though I tried. And that brings me to what I learned about myself."

Grant's vivid, blue eyes held her captive, and she could discern in their depths the turmoil he'd felt as he'd struggled with his growing feelings for her. "I want you to know that I loved Christine with all my heart. Part of me always will," he told her with absolute candor. "So I felt disloyal to her when I started to fall in love with you. But as Bill pointed out to me once, Christine has been gone in everything but body for three years. Death just gave her the final release. Still, I struggled with my feelings for a long time, until I finally realized that I had to let go of the past and move on. The only thing we have with any certainty is today. And today is a great gift. One I don't want to waste."

He took a deep breath. "I'll admit that I'm still afraid we may have problems reconciling our lifestyles. But I can't imagine my life without you in it. I can't give you glamour or glitz, but I can give you my love. For always. And that brings me to my counter offer."

Reaching into the pocket of his jeans, he withdrew a small square box. He lifted the lid, revealing a simple but stunning solitaire nestled against a backdrop of black velvet.

"My offer comes with a salary of unlimited love, and a bonus of companionship and friendship. The perks include a cottage by the sea, lifetime job security and, perhaps, in time and with God's grace, children at our table." He took her hand again, and she could feel his trembling. Or was it her own hand that was unsteady, she wondered? "Morgan, I would be honored if you would accept this offer and become my wife."

As she looked into Grant's tender eyes, her own filled with tears. Morgan had known joy in her life. But nothing that compared to this. Her heart soared and she smiled, even as a sob caught in her throat.

Instead of answering, she reached up and

cupped his face with her hands, reveling in the love she saw there. As she lost herself in his adoring gaze, his eyes darkened, and she leaned toward him. A moment later he lowered his lips to hers, and Morgan knew that this moment was but a taste of the joy to come. That with this man, all of her tomorrows would be filled with a love and devotion that would prove steady and true all the days of her life.

Grant, too, was filled with joy. As he held Morgan in his arms, he knew that he was a man doubly blessed. He'd known heaven on earth once, with Christine. And now he was being given a second chance to experience the joy and fulfillment of a deep, abiding love. Morgan would leave her own unique mark on his life, just as Christine had. Their life as a couple would be different from what he'd known before. But it would be a good one, based on partnership, sharing and commitment.

When at last he pulled back, Morgan continued to cling to him. He smiled and traced the delicate curve of her jaw with a gentle finger.

"Is that a yes?" he asked.

It took her a minute to find her voice. "I think that would be a safe bet."

"And you won't have any second thoughts about giving up the job in New York?"

Instead of responding, she stood. At his questioning look, she reached for his hand. "Come with me."

She led him back to the cottage, onto the deck, and into the dining room, then pointed to the printer. "Take a look."

Curious, he went over and retrieved the single sheet of paper in the tray. As he scanned it, she saw a slow smile spread over his face. When he finished, he turned back to her. "When did you decide to turn them down?"

"On the plane, coming back. I suddenly realized that I didn't want that kind of life anymore. That I loved Seaside. And I loved you. I hoped, in time, that you might be ready to move on, that maybe you would be able to open your heart to love again. But even if you never did, I knew that this was where I wanted to be. So you never need to feel guilty about keeping me in Seaside. Because I was planning to stay, with or without you by my side. But I much prefer this option," she finished with a smile.

Grant put the piece of paper on the table and moved toward her. Once more he took her hand and led her outside to the deck, where they paused to gaze out over the azure expanse of the sea. And then he turned to her, took her left hand in his, and slipped the ring over her finger. For a moment she looked down at it, the sparkle dazzling in the brilliant morning sun. When she looked back up at Grant, she saw the same dazzling sparkle in his eyes, and knew it was reflected in hers, as well.

"I love you, Morgan," he said.

"I love you, too," she whispered.

Then he leaned toward her to seal their engagement with a kiss that hinted at what was to come. A kiss that promised sweet tomorrows and pledged their love as surely as the vows they would soon exchange before God. A kiss that told her she had come home at last. For always.

And as she lost herself in his embrace, Morgan sent a silent, heartfelt message to the woman whose bequest had been the catalyst for her new life, a life in which her work would always be important, but never at the expense of the things that really mattered. Faith. Family. And love. Most especially love.

Thank you, Aunt Jo.

Morgan gave the ad layouts she was reviewing for a client in Portland a final scrutiny. As usual, Kit had done a stellar job on the production, and Morgan knew the client would be pleased. Satisfied, she set them aside and glanced at her watch. Grant should be here any minute.

The sudden crunch of gravel from the front drive announced his arrival, and Morgan grinned. You could always count on Grant to be on time. In fact, you could count on him to keep any promise he made. How blessed she was to have him in her life!

She rose to greet him, pulling open the door just as he reached up to knock, and found herself in his arms. When he released her after a kiss, she smiled up at him, her hands still looped around his neck. "Now that's what I call a 'hello!'"

He grinned. "I could do even better if I wasn't juggling our lunch in one hand and your mail in the other."

She chuckled and stepped back. "Come on in. I'm starving!"

"So am I," he said with a wink.

The color rose in her cheeks and she felt her own pulse quicken. "The wedding's only three weeks away," she reminded him.

"That's three weeks too long," he countered, his eyes darkening. Then he took a deep breath and smiled. "But I'll cope. Let's eat out on the deck, okay?"

"I'll grab a couple of sodas."

When she joined him a few moments later, he handed her the mail. "Thanks," she said, setting the stack of envelopes aside as she focused on her food. "By the way, that architect you mentioned stopped by this morning. Matthew Lange."

"What did he say?" Grant asked as he unwrapped his sandwich and took a big bite.

"He didn't see any reason we couldn't expand the cottage. He's going to put together some preliminary ideas for our review."

"Great. I listed my house yesterday. I don't think I'll have any problem selling it."

Morgan's face grew thoughtful. "I wonder what Aunt Jo would think about us getting together and making Serenity Point our home?"

"I have a feeling she'd approve. And speaking of Jo, there's a letter from her attorney in your mail. I noticed the return address when I pulled it out of the box."

Shuffling through the mail, Morgan withdrew a long envelope from Seth Mitchell. "Do you mind if I open it?"

"Not at all. I'll just enjoy the view," he replied with a smile, keeping his gaze fixed on her.

Morgan's eyes softened and she smiled in return, reaching out to touch his face. He captured her fingers in his and kissed each one, never breaking eye contact. Not until he released her hand did she remember the envelope she was holding. She slit it and withdrew a single sheet of paper, as well as another smaller envelope.

"Dear Ms. Williams: Your aunt asked that I forward this to you after the six-month period stipulated in her will. My congratulations again to you and Mr. Kincaid. I wish you great happiness."

Setting Seth's note aside, Morgan turned her attention to the smaller envelope, which was addressed to her in her aunt's flowing hand.

"It's a note from Aunt Jo," she told Grant in surprise.

"Hmm. That's interesting. Go ahead and read it."

She pried open the smaller envelope, withdrawing two folded sheets of paper, and began to read.

My dearest Morgan,
If you are reading this, it means that you have fulfilled the stipulations in my will. You are either thanking me for enhancing your life or wishing all sorts of dire things on me for disrupting it. I hope it is the former.

I'm sure, when you first heard my requirements, you were not happy. And you probably thought that the residency provision would be impossible to meet, given your demanding job. But you have found a way to satisfy that condition. And for that I am glad. You have also served on the board of Good Shepherd, an organization that is dear to my heart. And knowing your talent and conscientiousness, I have every hope that your work there has reaped great benefits that will continue long after your six-month stint on the board.

My intent with these stipulations, dear Morgan, was not to disrupt your life. At least not in a negative way. But for some time I have been concerned that in your pursuit of worldly success, you have abandoned the things that matter most. Your faith, certainly. But also your sisters. They love you, nonetheless, but family is a thing to be cherished and nurtured, and I feared that someday those precious links would weaken and break from neglect.

I also worried about the lack of love in your life. Next to faith, love is the most sustaining, life-giving force in the world. Your uncle and I had a wonderful marriage, and I always hoped all three of my great-nieces would find that same kind of love, for it is a priceless treasure. But you never seemed to place much importance on marriage.

So, all of these concerns prompted the unusual stipulations in my will. By now you know Grant very well. And I hope that you have recognized what a wonderful man he is. His love for, and devotion to, his wife is a shining example of what a good marriage is all about. And his strong faith is an inspiration to all who know him, as are his selflessness and commitment to others. I have known Grant for many years, and I can say with all honesty that I have never met a finer man.

In my heart, I sense that there will come a time in the not-too-distant future when God will call Christine home. And when that happens, Grant will be alone. Knowing Christine's kind and generous spirit, I am sure she would not wish a life of solitude for the man she loved with such depth and fidelity.

Though you may not have seen it at the beginning, or perhaps even now, I think that—at heart—you and Grant have much in common. It is my hope that when the time comes, the two of you will share more than ownership of my simple cottage. But even if that is not to be, I am confident that your life will be enriched by knowing this special man. Through his example, I hope you come to understand the great gift that love offers, and that you will seek it in your own life.

Please forgive an old woman's meddling, my dear Morgan. Know that it was done with the best of intentions, out of a desire to leave you a far more lasting legacy than a mere cottage. Namely, love, grounded in faith and built on solid values. It is my fondest wish that you are on your way to finding that.

When—or if—the time is appropriate, feel free to share this note with Grant. And may God always keep you both in his tender care.

Aunt Jo.

As Morgan finished reading, she felt Grant's hand on her cheek. She closed her eyes and reached up to cover his strong fingers with her own, only then realizing that tears were streaming down her face.

"What's wrong?" he asked in concern.

She opened her eyes, and her heart overflowed with love and gratitude as she handed him the letter. He scanned it, and when he finished, his own eyes were damp.

"She was a very special lady," he said with a catch in his voice. "I miss her."

Morgan reached over and took his hand. "I have a feeling she'll always be with us in spirit," she murmured. "Especially here, in this place that she loved so much."

"I think you're right." Grant looked out over the blue sea, toward the distant lighthouse. "You know, Jo always found that lighthouse comforting. Even on the darkest, stormiest nights it shone like a beacon, guiding weary travelers home. Much like our faith does, she used to say. I'm glad it's out there, as a reminder, in case we ever lose our way."

"I agree." Morgan squeezed his hand, knowing that their life together wouldn't be all smooth sailing. No relationship, no life, escaped the occasional storm. But she wasn't afraid of the journey to come. With her rediscovered faith, and Grant by her side, she would always be safe.

Because she had already docked in her home port.

And she didn't intend to leave.

Epilogue

A.J. peeked out the window of the cottage and then turned to her sisters with a grin. "What a perfect day for a wedding!"

Morgan moved beside her sister and stole a quick look at the cerulean sea, the cloudless blue sky and the deep green pines that had become so familiar to her over the past few months. Then she scanned the guests assembled on the back lawn, seated in white folding chairs that faced the ocean. "And it looks as though the time is at hand."

Clare moved between her sisters, and a tingle of excitement ran down her spine. The setting was spectacular. All of the people they loved were on hand. And soon they would take the vows that would signal the start of a new life for each of them.

"You guys look fabulous."

The three brides turned to eleven-year-old Nicole, Clare's soon-to-be stepdaughter, as she gave each of them a long, appreciative look.

A.J. wore a vintage 1960s wedding dress in a gauzy fabric, with a square neckline, empire waist and long, flowing sleeves. Numerous hairpins made a valiant effort to tame her unruly strawberry blond hair, which was crowned with a wreath of daisies, and the matching daisies in her bouquet were interspersed with Maine wildflowers.

Morgan looked every inch the big-city bride in her strapless, satin gown topped with a short-sleeved bolero jacket. Her hair was pulled back on one side by a clip decorated with tiny fresh orchids and stephanotis, and she carried an exotic-looking bouquet of tropical flowers.

Clare had chosen a long, petal-colored chiffon dress that enhanced the faint blush on her cheeks and flowed gracefully when she moved. She wore a simple strand of pearls above the boat neckline, and had chosen pink roses and baby's breath for her bouquet.

"If I do say so myself, Nicole is right," A.J. declared with a grin. Then she turned to the young girl. "And our junior bridesmaid looks pretty good herself."

Nicole blushed and reached up in a self-conscious gesture to check her French braid, which had been twined with baby's breath. The spaghetti straps and fitted bodice of her mint-green dress showed off her developing figure, and the graceful waltz length allowed the shimmery fabric to swirl around her legs. "Clare did my hair. And she helped me pick the dress," Nicole said.

"Exhibiting her good taste, as always," Morgan noted, directing a smile to her older sister.

The string quartet struck up the opening chords of the prelude, and the gentle strains of "Jesu, Joy of Man's Desiring" drifted through the air.

A.J.'s eyes began to dance, and her grin grew even bigger. "I guess this is it."

"Any second thoughts?" Clare asked with a smile.

"Not a one. How about you two?"

Clare and Morgan looked at each other and shook their heads.

"Absolutely none," Clare said.

"I second that," Morgan added.

"I wish Aunt Jo could be here," A.J. said, her expression wistful.

Morgan smiled. "I have a feeling she is."

"Speaking of Aunt Jo…don't forget the roses, Nicole," Clare reminded her.

The young girl lifted the three yellow roses and laid them on her arm. "Is it time now?"

Clare nodded and leaned down to give her a hug. "You're on, sweetie."

The three sisters watched as Nicole made her way down the aisle, toward the platform that Andrew and Pete had constructed beside the sea. Bill, waiting there, gave her an encouraging smile as she approached.

A.J. moved into position. And as the strains of the bridal march began, she stepped outside and began her walk down the white runner.

While the sisters had agreed that Aunt Jo's cottage was the perfect setting for their weddings, Seaside was a long way from St. Louis. So A.J. hadn't expected many of her new friends to make the trip. But she was touched that George and Sophia Pashos had taken time off from their restaurant to come. And of course Jan, her fiancé's mother, was seated among the guests.

But A.J. wouldn't have cared if no one had come—except the man she loved. Blake was waiting in front for her, with his father beside him as his best man, and her heart overflowed. As their gazes met and held, she saw in his eyes the depth and promise of his love, and a pledge that it would be forever. A forever she had learned to believe in once again after learning to put her trust in the Lord.

As A.J. took Blake's arm, Morgan began her slow walk down the aisle. Though the crowd was small, most of the faces were familiar to her after her months in Seaside. Kit and the twins, Uncle Pete, Joe and Elizabeth Carroll, Sylvia and other Good Shepherd board members, along with Grant's many friends from town, all of whom she was getting to know. Even Grant's mother had made it into town for the wedding.

But, like A.J., Morgan focused on the man she loved. Grant, too, had chosen his father as his best man, and Andrew looked radiant. But not as radiant as his son. As Morgan looked into Grant's vivid blue eyes, she knew that their coming together was no less than a miracle. With God's grace, Grant had found the courage to overcome his fear and let go of the past, while Morgan had learned to value the things that really counted and to realign her life accordingly. And love had been their reward, a deep, enduring love that now shone in Grant's eyes and mirrored what was in Morgan's heart. A shining beacon that would sustain them for the rest of their lives, through good times and bad.

Morgan took Grant's arm as they moved beside the platform, then turned to watch Clare make her entrance.

Clare waited until Morgan was in place, then stepped onto the pristine runner. She knew few of the guests. But Adele Malone and her husband were there from North Carolina. And so was Adam's sister-in-law, Theresa, who was front and center—and keeping an attentive eye on her groom's niece and nephew, who were watching the proceedings with excited, wide-eyed excitement.

Clare gave Adam's best man—his brother, Jack—a quick smile, but then turned her attention to the tall, dark and handsome tuxedo-clad man beside him. The look of love and devotion on his face was enough to make her knees weak, and her heart swelled with emotion. Never had she expected to be given a second chance for happiness. Nor had Adam. But in His goodness, the Lord had looked on them both with kindness. And now, with faith in His abiding presence, they faced tomorrow with hope and confidence.

When Clare took Adam's arm, he laid his hand on hers and gave her a smile that filled her with joy. As they joined the group assembled at the base of the platform, Nicole stepped forward and handed each of the sisters a yellow rose.

A.J., Morgan and Clare moved together to an empty chair that stood slightly apart from the other guests. Beside it, on a small easel, rested an enlarged copy of the photo of Aunt Jo that Morgan had discovered in Grant's house. One by one, the sisters bent down and placed a rose on the seat in memory of the woman who had transformed each of their lives. Then they clasped hands and stood in silence, each paying tribute to the aunt who had left them a legacy beyond price.

A legacy of love.

And as the sisters—and brides—turned back to ascend the platform and recite the vows that would unite them with the three special men who had stolen their hearts, they each uttered the same, silent message.

Thank you, Lord. And thank you, Aunt Jo.

* * * * *

Dear Reader,

It is with mixed feelings that I finish this three-book series for Love Inspired, SISTERS & BRIDES.

On the one hand, I am ready to move on to something new. On the other, it is hard to say goodbye to the characters that have peopled my life for the past eight months.

But in a way, this transition mirrors life, which is a series of endings and beginnings, of saying hello and bidding farewell. In this final book, Grant must say goodbye to an old love before he can welcome a new woman into his life, just as Morgan must say goodbye to an old way of life before she can begin a new one. But with a little push from Aunt Jo, and by putting their trust in the Lord, both find the courage to follow their hearts and build a future together.

As you journey on life's often winding path, may the Lord always be with you, guiding your steps. And, with trust in His abiding presence, may you, too, find the courage to follow your heart and to look toward tomorrow with hope and joy.

Irene Hannon

SUSPENSE

RIVETING INSPIRATIONAL ROMANCE

Coming in November...

Her Brother's Keeper

by **Valerie Hansen**

An ordained minister turned undercover investigator is on a mission to uncover the truth about a young woman's past. But can he do that without hurting the woman he's come to love?

Available at your favorite retail outlet.
Only from Steeple Hill Books!

eHARLEQUIN.com

The Ultimate Destination for Women's Fiction

The ultimate destination for women's fiction.
Visit eHarlequin.com today!

GREAT BOOKS:
- We've got something for everyone—and at great low prices!
- Choose from new releases, backlist favorites, Themed Collections and preview upcoming books, too.
- Favorite authors: Debbie Macomber, Diana Palmer, Susan Wiggs and more!

EASY SHOPPING:
- Choose our convenient "bill me" option. No credit card required!
- Easy, secure, 24-hour shopping from the comfort of your own home.
- Sign-up for free membership and get $4 off your first purchase.
- Exclusive online offers: FREE books, bargain outlet savings, hot deals.

EXCLUSIVE FEATURES:
- Try Book Matcher—finding your favorite read has never been easier!
- Save & redeem Bonus Bucks.
- Another reason to love Fridays—Free Book Fridays!

Shop online
at www.eHarlequin.com today!

INTBB204R

Love Inspired

IN THE SPIRIT OF... CHRISTMAS

BY

LINDA GOODNIGHT

Jesse Slater was raising his traumatized little girl, trying to reclaim his family's farm...and dealing with bitter memories of past holiday seasons. He didn't count on falling for his temporary boss Lindsey Mitchell. Lindsey sensed there were reasons behind Jesse's lack of faith, and wondered if she was meant to teach him and his daughter the true meaning of Christmas....

Don't miss IN THE SPIRIT OF...CHRISTMAS
On sale November 2005

Available at your favorite retail outlet.